The Perfect Enemy

F. E. HIGGINS

NON-FICTION SECTION
BY CHRISTOPHER EDGE

ALWAYS LEARNING

PEARSON

Published by Pearson Education Limited, Edinburgh Gate, Harlow, Essex, CM20 2JE.

www.pearsonschoolsandfecolleges.co.uk

Text © F. E. Higgins 2012
Non-fiction text © Christopher Edge 2012
Typeset by Kamae Design
Cover photo © Akiyoko/Shutterstock

The rights of F. E. Higgins and Christopher Edge to be identified as authors of this work have been asserted by them in accordance with the Copyright, Designs and Patents Act 1988.

First published 2012

15 14 13 12
10 9 8 7 6 5 4 3 2 1

British Library Cataloguing in Publication Data
A catalogue record for this book is available from the British Library

ISBN 978 0 435 075347

Printed in China (CTPS/01)

Acknowledgements
We would like to thank Queensbridge School and students for their invaluable help in the development and trialling of this book.

To my Doppelgänger, wherever you may be …

Contents

Prologue

In the depths of a winter's night, in a nameless coastal town, a lonely figure came trudging through the snow that lay on the roads. He was pushing a small cart, its load covered by a dirty blanket. This was not an easy task uphill on the rough, icy ground. The snow had long been hardened by the boots of passers-by and the traveller was panting heavily at the effort. He stopped for a moment to push back a part of the load that was dangling over the edge of the cart and then trudged steadily on, like a beast of burden.

Soon he reached the top of the hill and entered the town square. He crossed it diagonally and turned off down Salter's Alley. He stopped under an old sign swinging on rusty chains. The peeling letters read:

The Smuggler's End
Tavern and Lodging House

The traveller knocked three times on the door, each knock as precise as the striking of the clock's hammer. There was no reply. He knocked again. A shout came from an overhead window.

'What's your game, lad? Can't you see we're closed? Come back in the morning!'

'But I got something for you,' the traveller called back, keeping his head down and muffling his voice with his scarf. 'Something important. There's money in it.'

The window slammed and the sound of heavy footsteps echoed down on the stairs. Moments later the door opened and revealed the generous form of Mrs Ena Harbledown. She stood there with a flickering chamber candle. The landlady peered at the traveller.

'This had better be worth it,' she snapped. Her sleep-creased face was no less ugly for the feeble light.

'Judge for yourself,' he said.

In one quick movement he pulled the cover from the cart to reveal its load. Mrs Harbledown leaned over to see and let out a screech of horror.

There in the cart, crumpled almost beyond recognition, lay the bloodied, broken and very dead body of a boy. The moon shone down on the boy's mud-green eyes. And the eyes reflected nothing.

Chapter One

Two days earlier …

'Aaaahhhh!'

Ralph Bennett stretched and yawned widely, watching his breath cloud in front of his mouth. He reckoned it was as cold this morning as it had been every morning for the last few weeks, if not colder. He'd had another disturbed night on account of the crashing and thumping from the room next door. The lodger, a knife-grinder in town for the Winter Fair, had been drinking late into the night in the tavern. Ralph had helped him up the stairs.

I wonder how he is today? Ralph thought as he knelt on his hard, lumpy mattress, reaching for the wall that divided his room from the next.

He pulled a cone-shaped piece of wood out of one of the wooden beams in the wall. When he closed one eye and put the other to the hole, he had a surprisingly good view of the next room. Only the corners to his left and right were out of sight. The knife-grinder's bed was empty.

He's gone early. I'd have thought he'd be sleeping it off.

Ralph chewed on his lip and frowned. This was the third time recently a lodger had taken his leave before sunrise. Once was of no importance; twice could be a coincidence. But three times?

'Ralph! You fed them pigs yet?' came the screeching call from the bottom of the stairs. Mrs Harbledown was up.

Ralph shuddered and swore softly, a familiar pang of fear arising at the sound of the woman's voice.

'Just coming,' he called back. 'You old bag,' he muttered under his breath.

He pushed back the wooden plug and slid off the bed. He winced as a sharp pain shot through his shoulder. Mrs Harbledown had violently wrenched his arm yesterday.

Because I hadn't swept the tavern floor to her satisfaction, he thought bitterly. *She cares no more for me than a master does his slave.*

The slave-driver herself, Mrs Harbledown, was waiting at the bottom of the stairs. Her feet were set apart and her fat arms crossed over her bulging stomach. Ralph expected to see her seams burst open at any moment. The thought turned his own, much leaner, grumbling stomach. Suddenly she grabbed him by the ear and twisted it.

'No time for lying about, boy,' she snarled. 'Them pigs need fattening up for slaughter.'

You're fat enough for slaughter, thought Ralph darkly.

She let go and he hurried away, ducking to avoid the back of her hand, which just grazed his head.

Outside, a freezing wind whipped around the yard and sliced like a cut-throat razor. It was coming off the sea from the north, and when Ralph licked his lips he could taste salt. For a moment he allowed himself to daydream about running away to sea. The grunting pigs brought him back to land.

Frozen to the bone, Ralph climbed over the fence and into the pen. He stumbled across the churned-up mud while the pigs watched him from the shelter of the hut that he had built.

'Not bad,' Ralph muttered. 'Considering the poor scraps of wood I was given to make it!'

He crossed to the old butler sink that held their drinking water and smashed through the icy surface with the heel of his boot. The pigs remained in their hut.

'Not hungry then?' he said.

They grunted and stayed put.

'Odd. Maybe it's too cold for you.'

Usually the pigs were butting the back of his legs, frantically trying to get to the slops. He banged on the side of the tin pail with a muddy stick. Still the pigs paid him no attention.

'Well I'm hungry, even if you're not,' he said, reaching into the slops for a couple of hard crusts that were sitting on top of the vegetable peelings.

'Harbledown prefers you pigs to people,' said Ralph as he munched. 'I swear, this is the last winter I spend in this place.'

But in truth, the thought of leaving was as terrifying as the prospect of staying.

As usual, the pigs had almost cleared the trough from the previous day. All that was left was a scattering of bits too small for them to pick up and a long ribbon of material. Ralph picked it out and held it up, waving it at the pigs.

'Now how did this get in there?'

It had once been red but now was grey. A rag from the kitchen? He discarded it and was about to empty today's food into the trough when he saw some small, yellowish pebbles in the bottom. Normally he wouldn't have given them a second thought, but for some reason the scrap of material had alerted his senses. He gathered up the pebbles from the trough and examined them in the flat of his palm. His guts churned. These weren't pebbles.

They were human teeth.

Chapter Two

Ralph's hands were still trembling when he returned inside. He could hear the sizzling of sausages from the kitchen. Normally the smell would have been mouth-watering, but the thought of what the pigs had been eating left him on the verge of retching.

Mrs Harbledown was talking and laughing with Fingers, the tavern's odd job man. Fingers was sporting a rather nice green waistcoat under his coat.

The knife-grinder wore a green waistcoat, thought Ralph.

He remembered it quite clearly from when he had helped the fellow up to bed. In a flash he recalled too how the fellow's red scarf had come loose and fallen on the stairs. The man had picked it up and clumsily stuffed it in his trouser pocket.

Fingers saw Ralph and gave Mrs Harbledown a nod. She turned around quickly, no trace of the smile left on her face. She advanced heavily towards him, her mouth twisted into a sneer, pointing her fat finger at him.

'What's up with you, boy?'

'N-nothing,' he stammered. 'But I wanted to know, when did he leave? The knife-grinder, I mean.'

Mrs Harbledown narrowed her eyes. Ralph thought she was going to hit him again and cowered. Instead she poked him in the chest, one prod with every word.

'What's it to you? Get up there and put his room to rights. There'll be more guests later.'

She lumbered away with Fingers in the direction of the kitchen. Ralph felt himself fill up with disgust and anger as he watched her retreat. In his pocket he turned the teeth over and over. There was no way a human tooth got into a pig trough by accident. And what about that waistcoat of Fingers' and the shredded red material? It all made sense now. The noises in the night, the early departures. It was almost too terrible to contemplate.

'You filthy wretches,' Ralph hissed after the pair. 'Enjoy your sausages.' He hurried away up to the knife-grinder's empty room.

Like his own room, the guest room was a small space with a tiny window in the sloping roof. It allowed in hardly any light, even when it wasn't covered in snow. Mrs Harbledown had provided as little furniture and comfort as was necessary for a guest not to object to the price of two shillings. Ralph closed the door and leaned against it. He knew he was safe here for the time being. Mrs Harbledown rarely came up the stairs. His breathing steadied but he couldn't rid himself of the fear that had settled in the pit of his stomach.

He tried to continue as if nothing had happened. He had done that before, after a beating or a tongue-lashing. He pulled up the worn blankets and pummelled the tired pillow. But all the while his mind was racing. He looked around, as he always did, in case the lodger had left something of value behind. It didn't feel right – not now that he knew about the knife-grinder's grisly death.

'I'm like a vulture at a carcass,' he said, disgusted with himself. But he continued his search. He didn't want to admit it, but he knew he was looking for blood, or signs of a struggle. Anything that might prove his terrible theory.

Maybe I should use what I know against the old witch, he thought spitefully.

He imagined how it would be, how he would tap Mrs Harbledown on the shoulder and tell her that he knew what she and Fingers were up to. He thought about the look on her face when she realised she had been rumbled. For a moment he was full of triumph.

But what then? he asked himself gloomily. *She'd laugh at me, beat me again and send me out onto the street.*

He was powerless. He couldn't risk his job, not in the winter. There were dozens of boys in the town who would snap it up, as Mrs Harbledown so often reminded him with a slap. Besides, what exactly did he know?

He had no real proof – the pigs had made sure of that. The constables would hardly believe him, a tavern boy.

They held Mrs Harbledown in high regard because she gave them free ale. He was struck by a worrying thought.

What if Mrs Harbledown thinks I do know something? Who's to say I won't be next in the trough?

Ralph's thoughts continued to leap from one grim scenario to another. It was not long before he concluded that he couldn't stay at the tavern any longer. He had fantasised about leaving many times, but never seriously. He had no special skills, no trade, and he was penniless. He rarely thought past the next chore. He had come to accept that he would never make much of his life. He had no ambition. Mrs Harbledown had beaten it out of him.

But that was before the teeth.

Mrs Harbledown has money, thought Ralph to himself. *She counts it up every night in the back room. Maybe I could take it.*

His eyes widened at the very thought of stealing from her.

She won't give it up without a fight. I'd have to sneak up on her, hit her over the head or something.

He shook his head. He couldn't do that! In self-defence, possibly, but in cold blood? Despair washed over him. Never had he felt so completely alone.

'Hello.'

Ralph jumped at the sound of the voice. A girl, about his age, was standing at the door. She was wearing a grey cloak with a hood and there was snow on her black boots.

'How did you get in?' he asked.

The girl stepped inside the room.

'There was no one around so I just came up. I'm Myrtle. I'm looking for my uncle. I believe he was staying here. He's a knife-grinder.'

'Oh. He's gone,' said Ralph slowly. 'I mean, he left early this morning.'

The girl looked puzzled.

'How odd. We met at the fair yesterday. He said for me to come here this morning. He was going to give me some money before he left town.' She looked around. 'Was this his room?'

'Yes.' Ralph was uneasy. The teeth were like lead weights in his pocket.

'You work here, do you?'

Ralph nodded and began to shepherd the girl out of the room.

'You should go. You'll get me into trouble.'

Myrtle looked concerned. 'I don't want to do that. Is she quite strict then, Mrs Harbledown?'

Ralph raised his eyebrows and managed a laugh.

'You could say that.' He led her onto the landing, hurried her down the stairs and took her to the tavern door.

'What's the rush?' asked Myrtle.

'It's Mrs Harbledown,' muttered Ralph.

Myrtle looked at him in surprise. 'Are you afraid of her?'

'No, of course not.'

Myrtle laughed. 'Yes you are. It's all over your face. Why don't you up sticks and go if she's that bad?'

'It's not that simple.'

Myrtle shrugged. 'It's as simple as you want it to be. Did my uncle say where he was going?'

'I didn't see him,' said Ralph truthfully. He could tell the girl was disappointed. 'I'm sorry. If he comes back I'll tell him you were here.'

'Thanks, anyway,' she said, looking at him kindly.

'Chin up. Worse things happen at sea!'

Ralph watched at the window as Myrtle walked away up the icy street. She looked back once, saw him and gave a wave and a smile. He couldn't remember the last time someone had smiled at him and meant it. He felt wretched at his lies.

But what could I say? By the way, I think your uncle has been eaten by a pig.

No, better she didn't know. Besides, he wasn't even completely sure yet.

But in reality, any hope he had that there was another explanation was as tattered as the knife-grinder's scarf.

Meeting Myrtle had unsettled Ralph almost as much as finding the teeth. She was right. It was simple. He couldn't stay any longer; therefore, the answer was to go. He spent the day mulling over his options, jumping every time Mrs Harbledown or Fingers appeared.

It was early evening and Ralph was on the stairs, still lost in thought, when he heard the street door open and someone come in. There was a man standing in the hall.

Ralph shivered violently. He had the oddest feeling that it wasn't the open door that let in the bitter chill of winter, rather that the man had physically brought it with him.

The newcomer was not tall, but somehow his shadow crept high up the walls. His ill-fitting coat just brushed the floor and the soles of his stained boots dragged noisily across the flagstones as he went towards the fire. Ralph strained to see the man's face but it was hidden by his matted hair and his hat, which he had pulled down low. It was as if the stranger didn't want to be seen.

The man reached under his coat and took out a small black box which he set down carefully on the stone hearth. He placed a foot on either side of it and held his hands out to the flames. Ralph could see that the box was made from wood, ebony he thought, and that it was highly polished. Its curved lid was carved around the edges and it was kept closed by two leather straps with brass latches and a brass lock. It looked something like a small pirate treasure chest, and Ralph was instantly curious about its contents. The man seemed keen to keep the box close to him.

Just then Mrs Harbledown appeared.

'Good evening, Sir,' she sneered in the voice she reserved for paying guests. 'Ralph should have told me you were here, useless boy that he is. You tell him to do one thing and he does the opposite. I'm Ena Harbledown, the landlady. Was it a room you wanted for tonight, or maybe two?'

'Just the one room, just the one night,' came the weary reply.

'Then you're in luck, Sir. I have a room, just vacated today. Small, but cosy, I say. It's two shillings, dinner included, and sixpence extra for breakfast. Sausages from my own pigs of course, and —'

The man silenced her by holding out a small purse of coins. Mrs Harbledown shook them out and counted, her lips moving as she did so. She turned her head in the direction of the stairs and opened her mouth to screech.

'I'm here,' said Ralph just in time.

'Take our guest …' she looked at the man expectantly.

'Doran,' said the man. 'Mr A. P. Doran.'

'… take Mr Doran up to the attic room.'

Mr Doran, the black box tucked under his arm, followed Ralph up the stairs. He climbed with difficulty, audibly puffing and knees cracking. Ralph waited on the landing, trying not to stare at the box, but he could hardly keep his eyes off it. This close, he could see that it really was quite special. It had to be worth a good amount. A plan began to form in his head, and dark thoughts whispered once more.

I could steal the box, sell it, and then run away.

Perhaps, for once, things were starting to go in his favour.

In the room, Ralph lit the fire while Mr Doran caught his breath. Ralph could feel the man's eyes boring into his back. He could smell dampness and something else, a sort of cloying sweetness. The kindling began to crackle.

'Well, I'll be off then,' said Ralph. He took one last lingering look at the box, still held in Mr Doran's grasp. Suddenly, overcome by a strange impulse, he reached out to touch it. Mr Doran leapt back like a scalded cat.

'No!' he shouted. 'Don't touch it!'

Startled at the ferocity of Mr Doran's reaction, Ralph retreated hastily.

'I … I … just wanted to …' he stuttered. 'I mean, would you like me to look after it for you? I could put it somewhere safe, under lock and key downstairs. It looks valuable.'

'No value can be placed on this … box,' growled Mr Doran. 'And I do not wish to give it over to you. I warn you, lad – you try to touch it again, it'll be the worse for you.'

Tucking the box tightly under one arm, the man used his free hand to steer Ralph firmly out of the room and close the door. Ralph stood on the landing, his mind made up. He *had* to have that box!

Chapter Three

'So, Ralph, what's in the box?' asked Mrs Harbledown as soon as he reached the hall.

Ralph took a step back. He felt a sharp sting of disappointment; he had hoped she hadn't seen the box.

'Dunno,' he shrugged sullenly. 'He wouldn't even let me touch it.'

Mrs Harbledown sniffed suspiciously.

'You ain't lying to me, are you? It's something important, I know. You can tell from the way he held it.'

'And I'm *telling* you, he wouldn't let me near it,' retorted Ralph, with unusual venom. 'It doesn't look like anything special to me.'

Mrs Harbledown snarled and took hold of his collar, twisting it tightly around his neck as if to strangle him. He cowered helplessly in her hold.

'Don't cheek me, Ralph Bennett,' she hissed. 'Or you'll be sorry.'

For the rest of the evening Ralph could think of nothing but the gleaming box. He was consumed by the thought of owning it. It was no longer just a box – now it was the key to his freedom! But Mrs Harbledown seemed to know something and she kept an even sharper eye on him than usual. As for Mr Doran, no one had seen him all evening.

It was midnight when Ralph finished work in the tavern. He raced up to the attic, pulled out the knot and peered through. Mr Doran was in bed with his arms out over the covers. The blanket rose and fell to the sound of his heavy breathing. The mysterious object of Ralph's obsession was gleaming on the bedside table. Ralph saw how the polished surface reflected the red embers of the fire and the way the buckles shone. The sight quickened his pulse.

What treasures it must contain!

Something glinted around Mr Doran's exposed neck. It was a key on a string.

'Rats,' muttered Ralph. 'It's for the box. It has to be. I'll have to take that as well.'

He rested back on his heels. He felt an odd mixture of fear and exhilaration.

'I *can* do this,' he whispered.

Moments later he eased open his neighbour's door and stepped inside. He was shaking, hardly able to believe what he was doing. His eyes were fixed on the polished box. In three swift steps he was at the bed. He took out his knife and reached for the string. He was just at the point of cutting it when Mr Doran turned his sleeping face towards him. Ralph gasped at what he saw and almost dropped the knife.

Mr Doran was old, older than anyone Ralph had ever seen. So old in fact that he thought he should be dead. He certainly looked dead, all dried up like some rotting animal you would find in the roof. The top of his head was completely bald and spotted with brown patches. The wild grey hair that stuck out from under his hat stopped above his ears, encircling his head like a white wreath. His skin was paper-thin and here and there it was visibly flaking. His eyes were ringed with dark circles. His lips were pale, almost blue, and his cheeks had sunk so far into his face that you could almost see the outline of his teeth in his jaw. And what teeth! Long and yellow and broken.

Just get the key, thought Ralph.

With great care he picked up the string between thumb and forefinger, held it taut over the blade and sliced through it. The key was his!

With a wide grin he grabbed the box and crept out, concentrating too much on getting back to his room unnoticed to see that the box let off a soft glow the moment his fingers touched the gleaming wood.

Back in his own room, elated by his daring, Ralph examined the box properly by the lantern. It was a remarkable piece of craftsmanship. The joins were invisible and the finish was as smooth as a pebble on the beach. The carvings, small as they were, showed scenes of incredible detail.

Ralph ran his trembling fingers over the glossy surface. It was cool to the touch and seemed to set off a tingling in his fingers. To his delight, he noticed that no matter how he stroked it, he left no marks on its gleaming surface. He shook it violently. The buckles rattled, but it did not sound as if there was anything inside. Finally, with fumbling fingers, he unbuckled the straps. As he pushed aside the brass disc that covered the keyhole he saw that there was an inscription on it.

Who turns this key, in one breath,
Will meet himself, and oft his death

'To hell with that!' Ralph laughed aloud and pushed in the key.

Instantly a tremendous noise came from behind him. The door flew open and Mr Doran crashed into the room, fear in the yellowing whites of his eyes.

'DON'T OPEN THE BOX!' he roared.

But it was too late. Startled by the commotion, Ralph flinched. The key turned, almost by itself, and the box flew up into the air and landed across the room on the floor, the lid wide open.

'NO!' shouted Mr Doran, reaching out desperately with his skeletal arms before collapsing to his knees.

There was a swooshing noise, like a strong gust of wind. Ralph felt as if the breath had been knocked out of him by a powerful blow to his chest. He was aware that he was falling and then everything went very quiet.

When Ralph opened his eyes he was lying on his back looking up at the cobwebs on the ceiling. He could see a spider spinning its web. He was close to the fire – one side of his body was warm and the other side was cold. His head was filled with noise like a swollen river rushing over the edge of a cliff. As it faded he sat up.

Nearby Mr Doran was getting slowly to his feet, the way old people do. He went to close the door and then sat on the bed. Ralph thought he looked as close to death as a man could be while still breathing.

He saw the black box at his feet and instantly remembered what he had tried to do. He was horrified. Stealing from a lodger, and for his own benefit? What if Mrs Harbledown found out?

'Hell and damnation!' Ralph croaked. 'I must be mad!'

Quickly he picked up the box and held it out to Mr Doran. He knew he had to give it back, but as he gazed at the polished surface he felt his fingers tighten. He was strangely reluctant to actually hand it over, and not just because he had convinced himself that it held the key to his freedom. He shook his head to break the trance-like feeling. Right now all he cared about was that Mrs Harbledown didn't find out what he had tried to do.

The old man stared at him with accusing eyes but made no effort to take the box.

'Mr Doran, here's your box back. I'm sorry for taking it, but no harm done. Forgive me, please, I don't know what came over me. Please don't tell Mrs Harbledown. She'll beat me black and blue.'

Mr Doran laughed bitterly.

'Ah, Ralph,' he said finally. 'If I could take it back, believe me, I would, but I can't. You touched it. It belongs to you now. I've had it far longer than I ever should have. I knew the time would come when I would have to pass it on. I am not in good health. I delayed in my duty as long as I could and now the choice has been taken from me.'

'Duty? What do you mean?' asked Ralph.

Mr Doran sighed heavily.

'I must say that I didn't expect it to be someone so young. I can forgive you, boy, for what you have done, but your actions cannot be undone. There is only one way forward: you must kill it or be killed.'

Ralph thought he had misheard.

'Kill what?'

Mr Doran leaned forward.

'The Doppelgänger,' he hissed. 'Your Doppelgänger. You've set it free, and it's coming for you.'

Chapter Four

'My doppel-what?' asked Ralph sceptically. 'What the hell is that?'

Mr Doran was sweating visibly and Ralph noticed that he kept looking at the door, as if expecting someone to come through it.

'Don't you know, boy?'

'No,' said Ralph impatiently. 'Should I?'

Mr Doran shook his head.

'I suppose not. Most people go through their whole life and never meet one. And it might have been that way for you too, if you hadn't stolen from me.'

'I said I was sorry.'

Ralph fastened the lid of the box, locked it and slipped the key in his pocket. It was his now, after all. A small glimmer of hope began to surface. Maybe all was not lost. Maybe he could still get away.

'Just tell me what you are talking about,' he said impatiently. Knowing his luck Mrs Harbledown or Fingers could come in at any second.

Mr Doran looked into the distance.

'Doppelgängers – "Double-walkers" they call 'em. You could say it's a person, for want of a better word. It looks like you, walks and talks like you, but believe me, lad, it ain't you. They have no loyalty, not even to other Doppelgängers, and they'll do anything, *anything*, to survive.'

'A double? That sounds like a twin, and I don't have one of them.'

'A twin, yes. Someone who, in appearance at least, is the spitting image of you. But that's where it ends. It ain't a person. It ain't even human. Lord knows where it comes from. Hell, maybe. It has no soul, no conscience to stop it. And its heart, if it even has one, is filled with pure evil.'

He laughed; a high pitched, almost hysterical laugh.

'I reckon they should be called "Double-talkers" cos there's not a word comes out of their mouths that ain't a lie. Don't listen to it. It'll confuse you, muddle your thoughts. It will say you have no chance against it, because it knows you inside out.'

Ralph was momentarily silenced. The old man's desperate tone was unsettling him. He frowned.

'But if it's mine,' he said slowly, 'then what's it doing in your box?'

Mr Doran let out a short exclamation.

'Now there's the thing. The Doppelgänger belongs to whoever is in possession of the box. So as soon as the box is passed on …'

Ralph was one step ahead of Mr Doran.

'Are you saying that when I took the box, the doppel thing inside became mine?'

'Yes.'

'Then there should be a warning or something. You should have told me.'

Mr Doran wagged a long, twisted finger.

'Now, Ralph, let's not forget, I told you clearly not to touch the box. If the fault lies anywhere, it's with you. And there is a warning. Didn't you see it?'

Ralph thought of the inscription.

'Yes, I read it, but it's hardly clear. You should have told me the reason not to open it.'

'Why? Was it so hard to take me at my word? If I said not to jump off a cliff, would you still do it unless I gave you a reason?'

'That's different,' muttered Ralph. 'What if I give the box back to you, then it'll be your Doppelgänger again.'

Mr Doran shrugged.

'Too late. My Doppelgänger ain't in there. Mine is dead.'

'Dead?'

'I killed it, Ralph, and that is what you must do to yours. It'll be back, to kill you. That's its only purpose. It cannot exist alongside you so it needs rid of you, to take over your life.'

'My life? It's welcome to it,' said Ralph with a short laugh. 'Working all hours for pennies and insults, having my ears torn off by Mrs Harbledown's razor tongue. Hah, she'd soon sort out your Doppelgänger.'

Mr Doran looked very troubled.

'Boy, this ain't no joking matter. You need to think fast and be alert day and night, if you are to survive. It'll …'

Mr Doran's voice suddenly seemed very far away. Ralph was having great difficulty taking this all in. He was not very superstitious. He didn't walk under ladders and if he spilled salt he threw it over his shoulder. But he didn't believe in ghosts or monsters or spooks in the dark. So why should he believe in an evil double in a box? Yet he could see the fear on Mr Doran's face and hear the scraping of his dry skin as he wrung his hands. Whether these Doppelgängers existed or not, Mr A. P. Doran certainly believed they did.

All right, he'd play along, if only to get it over and done with. Then he could still get away.

'Okay, let's say for a moment that what you're telling me is true.'

Mr Doran looked slightly less anxious, as if relieved that Ralph was finally beginning to pay attention.

'Good, good!' said the old man. 'But it won't be easy. The vile creature will not rest until it has brought about your death. It's like a dog with a bone. It's violent, it can't feel regret, or sorrow, or any of the emotions that make us human. But it delights in your pain. It don't care what it has to do to win. And when it gets bored of playing games, it'll rip you apart, limb from limb.'

Ralph held his hands up in a gesture of surrender.

'All right, so the Doppelgänger's not my friend. But how do I kill it? I don't even know where it is.'

Mr Doran laughed bitterly.

'Hah! Don't worry about finding it. It'll find you. So you have to be ready. Best not to sleep until you kill it. And remember, first chance you get, brand it.'

'Brand it?'

'Mark it, any way you can, so others can tell the two of you apart. And then stab it through the heart. Don't be afraid to give it a twist for good measure.'

He reached under his waistcoat. 'Here, have my dagger. It's always served me well, but now it's yours.'

He pulled a long dagger from the belt of his trousers and held it out, but Ralph never got to take it. At that instant the door exploded inwards and a swift-moving blur entered the room. In a split second it had wrenched the dagger from Mr Doran, pushed him away and stood right in front of Ralph. Though its face was in a shadow, Ralph could feel it staring straight into his eyes. It raised its arm and Ralph saw the shining blade slicing through the air towards him.

'No!' he shrieked and jumped back, tripping over his own feet and falling heavily onto the logs piled up on the hearth. He felt desperately for one of the scattered logs, grabbed it and threw it wildly at the figure, not quite believing what was happening. But the intruder seemed to know it was coming and neatly sidestepped it. The log smashed against the door jamb and bounced out onto the landing. The intruder stood over him now, the dagger raised, and Ralph put his arm across his eyes, unable to look any more.

But the blow he was expecting never came. With a cry Mr Doran leapt at the dark assailant and the two struggled fiercely. Ralph scrambled to his feet but it was too late. Mr Doran grunted twice and fell forward against Ralph. Together they tumbled to the floor. Out of the corner of his eye Ralph saw the attacker run from the room.

Ralph lay under Mr Doran's weight. He could feel a strange warmth creeping across his chest. There was an odd sound, a gurgle, coming from Mr Doran. His face was contorted and his eyes were rolling in his head. He looked at Ralph pleadingly.

Ralph eased himself out from under the frail man's boney frame.

'It's okay. He's gone,' he said. 'You must have scared him off.'

He hooked his hands under Mr Doran's armpits and dragged him onto the bed. It was like lifting a child. He picked up the overturned lantern and relit it.

'Blimey,' he said aloud.

There was blood all over Mr Doran's shirt. He was paler than ever but now his skin had a green tinge. Ralph opened his shirt and found the wound from the dagger. He tried to stop the blood flow with the blanket.

'I think it was a burglar,' said Ralph. 'I'll get Mrs Harbledown. You need help.'

'That weren't no burglar, lad,' whispered the old man. 'That was it! The monster I been tellin' you about.'

Ralph's eyes widened. 'You mean my Doppelgänger?'

Mr Doran nodded weakly. 'It's playing with you, boy. They like a fight. But it'll get you in the end. Don't even try to leave town; you won't make half a mile before it's upon you.'

Ralph pressed harder on the cloth but it was already soaked through. The man's life was oozing away.

'Stab it, you said. Is that what you did to yours?'

Mr Doran's body jerked upwards, gripped by a muscle spasm. His lips were moving but his voice was now barely a whisper. 'Yes, straight though the heart. Ain't no secret to it, you must fight it, with everything you have,' rasped the time-ravaged man. 'Now leave me be, I'm done for. Time to think of yourself. Kill it or become it, Ralph …'

Mr Doran exhaled long and loud and sank back onto the bed, his blank eyes staring at the ceiling. Ralph shook the old man's arm but he knew it was hopeless. With his thumbs he closed the wrinkled eyelids and stepped away from the bed. The lantern's gentle glow shone down over a grim spectacle; a scene of violence and chaos. Ralph looked around his small room in disbelief.

'So much blood!' he murmured.

He picked up the box, the cause of his misfortune, and saw that it had escaped untouched. He felt something underfoot, Doran's bloody dagger, so he scooped it up. Just then a broad shadow fell across him. With a yell he jumped back, swinging the dagger wildly.

'What in heaven's name is going on up here?' asked Mrs Harbledown furiously and breathlessly. 'Sounds like blue murd—'

She didn't finish her sentence because that was when she saw Ralph standing over the dead body of Mr Doran, clutching a bloody knife and clinging to the black box. She screamed so loudly that Ralph's ears rung.

'MURDER!' she screeched. 'MURDER!' and she ran from the room.

Chapter Five

Ralph ran to the door. He could hear Mrs Harbledown thundering down the stairs shouting at the top of her voice.

'Fingers! Ralph's gone and done in one of me guests! He's murdered Mr Doran!'

Ralph backed into the room, shaking with fear.

'She thinks I did it. What am I going to do now?' he gasped.

Ralph's great plan to escape had suddenly turned into a living nightmare. He felt sick. What little courage he had felt was long gone.

'Yes, what are you going to do Ralph?'

Ralph whirled around at the sound of the mocking voice.

'Where are you?' he shouted. 'Show yourself, you wretch!'

The assailant stood in the doorway, but in the dim light Ralph couldn't see him properly. Ralph stood his ground, though his legs were shaking, the dagger wobbling in his hand and the box tucked under his arm. The attacker advanced towards him, his pale face emerging from the shadows. He was no more than a boy.

'Hello, Ralph,' he said. 'Good to meet you at last.'

Ralph stared in horror and his stomach flipped violently.

'No!' he whispered. 'It's not possible. You're … you're me!'

The boy who faced him was, in every respect, Ralph himself. He was the same height and the same build: broad across the shoulders, with long legs. His hair was the same dark brown colour, with that infuriating cowlick on the forehead, slightly to the right. He was wearing the same clothes. And the two of them were looking straight into each other's matching mud-green eyes.

But it was the face that alarmed Ralph the most. It was like looking into a mirror, yet it was different.

Of course! he thought in an odd moment of clarity amongst the chaos. *In a mirror it wouldn't be reversed, my right eye would be directly opposite. For once, I am actually seeing my own face the way everyone else does.*

He was utterly mesmerised by this sinister double. He could see his slightly crooked mouth and how his left eyebrow was arched slightly higher than his right. He could also see the scar under his chin from the time Mrs Harbledown had pushed him down the stairs. The chipped front tooth from when she had hit him across the face with her rolling pin. There too was the scar on his wrist from when Fingers had held his hand on the stove's hot plate. Ralph wanted to reach out and touch the boy, to determine if he was real or just an apparition, but he was deterred by the evil look on his face, a look he hoped had never crossed his own.

'What do you want?' Ralph asked, surprised at how confident he sounded. In reality he felt as if his very bones had melted.

The boy smirked and replied in mock surprise.

'Why, Ralph, you know what I want. Surely Mr Doran told you before he so tragically passed away.'

Ralph shook his head in bewilderment. This was without doubt the most grimly peculiar thing that had ever happened to him.

'You … you murdered Mr Doran. The constables'll have you for it. You'll be hanged.'

The Doppelgänger merely shrugged.

'I think not. Enjoy your freedom while you can, Ralph. It won't last long.' And he was gone.

Ralph stood in shock in the dimness of the room.

But I thought he was meant to kill me.

He looked at the bloody dagger in his hand and was repulsed by it. He sank to the floor, trembling violently, confused by a series of clashing emotions.

Footsteps on the stairs jolted him back to reality. Cautiously he went out on to the landing. The Doppelgänger was nowhere to be seen, but Mrs Harbledown was below talking loudly and excitedly.

'The old man's been stabbed; Ralph done it. I saw him with my own eyes. He's still up there – you'll get him if you hurry. He ain't got nowhere to go. Watch yourself; he's got a big knife.'

'Don't you worry, Ena.' It was Fingers. 'He'll not escape me.'

Would they believe him? Not likely! Slipping the dagger into his belt, Ralph ran to his room and pushed the chair up against the door. It wouldn't hold for long – the hinges were hanging off. He grabbed his haversack, already packed with his few belongings, and stuffed the black box in the top. Then, unable to look Mr Doran in the face, he went through the dead man's pockets searching for anything that might help him. He found only a few sixpence pieces and a box of matches. He took the string from Doran's neck, put the key back on it and placed it over his own head. After all the terror and chaos the box had caused, Ralph was not going to let the key get lost. He would have taken the old man's boots as they were in better condition than his own, but there was something about tugging boots off a dead man that didn't seem right. Finally he grabbed the lantern.

'Now to get out of here!' he said nervously.

He jumped up on the bed, one foot either side of the cooling body, and pushed hard on the window. It was frozen shut. He could hear Fingers pounding on the door.

'C'mon, c'mon!' he urged himself.

He gave an almighty shove and the window came free with a sudden jerk. He lobbed the haversack through and then pulled himself up and out onto the icy roof. It was a short crawl to a hiding place behind the chimney stack.

There was a crashing sound from below and Fingers' voice floated into the silent night through the open window.

'Well the old man's had it, that's for sure.'

'But where's the box?' asked Mrs Harbledown.

'The boy must have taken it with him. He'll be well gone by now. I ain't going on to that roof.'

'Thieving toerag! I knew it was valuable. Probably full o' gold. I told you we should have gone up earlier.'

Fingers laughed.

'Well, well. I didn't think the runt had it in him. He's such a snivelling little coward. You know, I'd give him a pat on the back if he was here.'

Ralph's cheeks burned. A snivelling little coward. Is that what they thought of him? And it was hardly a compliment to earn Fingers' admiration. Mrs Harbledown, naturally, was not quite so impressed.

'I'd tan his hide and throw him to the pigs,' she said furiously. 'Look at the mess in here. I can't let this room with blood all over the floor. That boy was always more trouble than he was worth. And after all I did for him, this is the thanks I get.'

Behind the chimney stack Ralph gritted his teeth.

All you did for me! What about all I did for you, you … you …! Words failed him. In that instant he realised just how much he hated Mrs Harbledown, and the strength of that hatred scared him.

At last Mrs Harbledown and Fingers felt they had stared sufficiently long at Mr Doran's body.

'Don't worry, Ena,' Ralph heard Fingers say. 'Maybe the boy's done us a favour. People were getting suspicious. There was a young girl hanging about today, looking for the knife-grinder. Now we can blame the boy for all the disappearances, kill two birds with one stone. We'll get the constables on to him. He'll be thrown in the clink and hanged, like as not, and we can carry on as before. I quite fancy another waistcoat.'

'Heh, heh,' laughed Mrs Harbledown. 'Couldn't have thought of a better plan myself. Shame about the box. I don't suppose we'll ever see that again, but there's plenty more fish in the sea.'

All went quiet. Ralph, clinging to his precarious perch, was furious at what he had heard.

And why exactly am I running? I haven't committed a crime. I'm the one who should be going to the constables.

But now that Fingers and Mrs Harbledown planned to pin it all on him, he was painfully aware that trying to explain his story to the law was not a smart thing to do.

'What could I possibly say?' he wondered aloud, 'that wouldn't get me locked up or thrown into the asylum?'

He wasn't entirely sure which of the two was worse.

'If Mrs Harbledown and Fingers accuse me, I've no chance. But on the other hand, if I were in prison, I'd be safe from my Doppelgänger. At least until they hang me!'

Either way, he was the loser. The black box had started a chain of events that had set his miserable life on a very different course. His best chance now was to leave town, and fast.

With great care Ralph crossed the steep, icy rooftops, dislodging more than a tile or two. He listened to them crashing to the ground and prayed that they wouldn't draw anyone's attention. When he thought he was far enough away from the tavern, he took advantage of a rusty drainpipe and half-climbed, half-slithered down to the street. Then off he ran, keeping close to the walls and always looking over his shoulder.

'I suppose I've sort of got what I wanted,' he said to himself. 'I can't go back to the Smuggler's End now.'

But what exactly lay ahead?

Chapter Six

Presently Ralph reached the river, a ribbon of darkness flowing silently through the town, and he began to feel more hopeful.

'I'll go to the harbour and board a ship,' he decided. 'And hide until we're out at sea. And then they won't be able to send me back.'

Keeping close to the embankment wall, he made for the bridge that spanned the river a little further ahead. On the other side he could see the moonlit silhouettes of the packet ships – some unloading, some loading, yet all holding the promise of a new life. But then, to Ralph's dismay, he heard angry shouting and shrill whistles behind him.

'Damn! The law already!'

He broke into a run and came to a set of stone steps leading down to the water. The tide was out and he skipped across the squelching mud to the first arch of the bridge, where he hid in the dark. He pulled down his hat, pulled up his collar and tightened his coat around him, trying to blend into the dark night.

The whistles and shouts came very close, peaked and began to fade. Ralph allowed himself to relax. He would stay a little longer, just to make sure they were gone. He stifled a yawn, remembering that Mr Doran had said to stay awake until he found the Doppelgänger.

'The Doppelgänger!' he exclaimed. In all the chaos of the escape he had almost forgotten the very reason he had fled in the first place.

'Hah! And where exactly is this Doppelgänger? The way Mr Doran was talking I'd have thought he would have shown himself again by now.'

Ralph glanced at his haversack and saw that one corner of the box was sticking out. He hesitated. Was it safe to open it again? Surely the damage had already been done. He pulled it and the key out and unlocked it for the second time that night.

The lantern's dim light seemed to be swallowed up by the dark interior of the box and Ralph had to hold it up to see if there was anything else inside. It was disappointingly empty. He put his hand in to feel the velvety lining and ran it around the inside of the lid. He could feel an inscription. He looked harder and could just make out the words:

Surrender, become me, or die!

Ralph frowned as he read it aloud. 'Surrender? Become me?' This was not helpful.

A day ago, hours ago, he would have laughed at the very idea of this Doppelgänger. Even now he wanted to believe that he was the victim of a coincidence: an unlikely coincidence, but a coincidence all the same. It was not beyond the bounds of possibility that there could be another boy in existence who looked like him.

Out in the dark, shadowy night, however, it was not quite so easy to explain away what had happened. There still remained the fact Mr Doran was well and truly dead. The image of his bloodied body was a memory that would haunt Ralph for a long time. And as if to remind him, the dagger's sharp blade dug into his leg and he pulled it out from his belt. He could smell the blood on the blade. With a snarl of disgust he dipped the blade into the water and wiped it off on the seaweed that clung to the arch. Perhaps he should throw it away; it was the murder weapon after all. But he knew he would need all the help he could get.

The sight of the blood had unnerved him. Ralph could feel his newfound confidence wavering, but he mentally steeled himself.

The ships are so close and all I have to do is get to one. That Doppelgänger, or boy, or whatever he is, won't find me there.

He stuffed the box back in the haversack and replaced the key around his neck. Somewhere nearby a clock chimed. It would be light in a few hours. The thought cheered him slightly. He made his way cautiously back up onto the embankment and headed for the harbour. His nerves were raw and even the slightest noise startled him: a yowling cat streaking across the road, a whining dog, even an icicle dropping from a window. Again and again, like a nervous tic, he glanced anxiously behind him. Was it his imagination or could he hear footsteps? He stopped. All was silent, but his pulse quickened with fear.

Ralph ducked down an alley. It stank of rot and decay. A sailor was lying up against the wall, snoring. He stepped over him and hurried on. He was surprised to hear faint singing and laughing. An orange glow came from a doorway beneath a sign that read:

The Spicy Fish Inn

Relishing the thought of warmth and safety, Ralph pushed open the door and went in. It was a small enough place, comfortingly dark, and clearly a popular late-night haunt. Young and old men – mainly sailors – were crowded round the tables. They drank heartily from tall pewter tankards. It was clear from their snarling threats and dark looks that many were engaged in card games of a deadly serious nature. The air was full of choking tobacco smoke and the walls rang with shouts, threats and laughter. In one corner two men were arm-wrestling, cheered on by a small crowd. In another, by sound rather than sight, Ralph guessed there was a cockroach race in progress.

He squeezed through the crowd, picking up a small three-legged stool on the way, and settled in a corner. His senses were heightened, perhaps by fear and uncertainty, or perhaps it was just the odour of the place – Gin and beer, sweat and spice, and fish mingled together to create an atmosphere thick enough to cut with a knife. And there were plenty of knives around.

Suddenly, there was a chorus of shushing and all heads turned towards the far side of the tavern. Ralph couldn't see over the drinkers' heads but he heard a piano start up, and then a clear voice floated through the smoky air. Soon the whole place was singing along.

Ralph knew the song – a drinking song he had heard many times in the Smuggler's End. The singer sounded young, and he pushed through the crowd to get a better look. He was right: a girl, about his age, was standing at the piano. She sang with poise and confidence beyond her years.

You would need it here, thought Ralph looking at the drunken faces of the audience.

The girl turned her head and caught his eye. She seemed to start but then gave him a smile and a wink.

'Myrtle,' breathed Ralph, and for some reason he felt immediately better.

When the song was over, Myrtle acknowledged the clapping with a curtsey and then came straight over to Ralph.

'Hello, again,' she said brightly. 'Did you take my advice then?'

Ralph knit his eyebrows. 'Advice?'

'To take off from the Smuggler's End.'

'Oh, yes. I'm planning to go to sea. I thought this would be the place to come looking for work.'

'Finally had enough of those pigs,' she laughed.

Ralph couldn't help but snort.

'Not just the pigs. Mrs Harbledown and Fingers.'

'Fingers? That horrible little man I spoke to? He really was very rude to me. I don't suppose my uncle came back? It was pure luck that we met at the fair, but I can't believe he would disappear like that. Not without even leaving a message.'

Ralph fingered the teeth still in his pocket. This wasn't the time to share his suspicions.

'Er, no, he didn't come back. Maybe he forgot.'

Myrtle sighed and her face fell.

'Shame. I could do with the money he promised me. They cheer a lot here but I don't get paid much. And the place stinks.' She winked. 'But I hear there's a job going at the Smuggler's End.'

'No!' answered Ralph harshly. Then, seeing the surprised look on Myrtle's face, he softened his tone and explained. 'Mrs Harbledown is a dreadful woman. She and Fingers … they … they are just horrible,' he finished lamely. 'Believe me, you don't want to work there.'

Ralph was looking over her shoulder. There was a young fellow nearby. He had his back to them, but there was something about him … could it be? The fellow turned around and Ralph breathed a sigh of relief. Too old.

'I was only joking,' said Myrtle, giving him a friendly pat on the shoulder. 'Looks like they put you through hell.'

Ralph flinched at her touch.

'What? Sorry. I thought I saw someone I knew,' he stammered. 'Oh, never mind.'

'Are you all right? You seem uneasy.'

Ralph forced a smile.

'I think I should go to the harbour now, if I'm going to find myself a ship before dawn.'

'I'll walk with you,' said Myrtle, not even thinking to ask if that was all right with Ralph. 'I'm not singing again tonight and it's on the way home.'

Ralph nodded, quite pleased at the prospect of Myrtle's company, and waited while she fetched her cloak. Together the two of them pushed through the crowd to the tavern door. Myrtle stepped out on to the street but Ralph hung back.

'What is it?' she asked, a puzzled look on her face.

'I thought I saw someone.'

Myrtle stood with a hand on one hip and narrowed her eyes.

'Again? Are you in some sort of trouble?'

Ralph chewed on his lip.

'A little,' he admitted. 'Something happened at the Smuggler's End tonight.'

'What do you mean "happened"?'

'Well, there was er … a murder.'

Myrtle's eyes widened. For a terrible moment Ralph thought she was going to scream. In a panic he dragged her back into the doorway and clamped his hand on her mouth.

'Shhh,' he hissed. 'Just let me explain.'

But before he had the chance, Myrtle stamped hard on his foot and pushed him backwards. She whipped around and grabbed him by the arm, his bad arm, twisting it and forcing him to the ground.

'A murder?' she asked coolly. 'So that's why you left.'

'Yes,' gasped Ralph.

Myrtle twisted his arm even more and Ralph realised she had misunderstood.

'But I didn't do it,' he said hastily. 'One of the lodgers was stabbed and now for some reason I think the murderer is after me.'

No need to go into all that Doppelgänger business. But if you're going to lie, keep as close to the truth as possible, thought Ralph.

'Oh,' said Myrtle, and relaxed her grip somewhat. 'So what, the murderer is after you because he thinks you saw too much?'

'That's just it,' agreed Ralph, nodding rapidly. 'I did see too much. Far too much! But I didn't do it. Look, I don't expect you to trust me or believe me. I mean, I hardly know you.'

Myrtle released her hold and Ralph straightened up.

'That's some grip you've got there,' he said, obviously impressed at Myrtle's strength.

'You learn fast in the Spicy Fish,' said Myrtle drily.

Ralph rubbed at his arm.

'Anyway,' he said, 'it's not me you should be worried about; it's Mrs Harbledown and Fingers. They —' He stopped.

Myrtle pounced on Ralph's hesitation.

'They what? Is this something to do with my uncle? If you know, you must tell me.'

Ralph screwed up his face in worry.

'I really didn't want to tell you this.' He took a deep breath and told her, as kindly as he could, of his suspicions. 'I found these teeth in the trough and part of his red scarf.'

Myrtle's face turned pale with shock at the sight of the teeth on his palm and then creased with suspicion. Her confidence was noticeably shaken.

'How do I know you're not just making this up to get yourself off the hook?'

Ralph shook his head. This was becoming too complicated. And it was holding him up. He had tasted freedom and didn't want to lose it again.

'I can't make you believe me. All I want is to get on a ship and sail away. Please, don't cause a fuss. Just let me go.'

He was embarrassed to hear his voice, almost pleading. It was like being with Mrs Harbledown all over again.

'I'm sorry,' said Myrtle quietly and stepped out of his way.

Ralph threw his haversack over his shoulder and went cautiously into the street.

'You never told me your name', said Myrtle.

Ralph opened his mouth to speak but an odd shiver ran up and down his spine.

Then a familiar voice said,

'His name is Ralph.'

It was the Doppelgänger.

Chapter Seven

'Hello, Ralph. Feeling the cold?'

Ralph was rooted to the spot. How could it be possible for the sound of a voice, an eerily familiar voice, to strike such terror into his very core? Slyly, he slipped his hand inside his coat for the dagger, grateful now that he had kept it. He pulled it out slowly, keeping it hidden behind his back as he turned around.

The Doppelgänger was standing there, a huge grin on his face. Ralph swallowed hard and marvelled again at the exact likeness. He even recognised his own slightly uneven stance, from years of ducking Mrs Harbledown's fist. But Ralph had a feeling that this boy would have hit back, not ducked.

Before he could say anything Ralph saw Myrtle come out onto the street. She looked from one boy to the other, surprise showing in her pale face.

'Why, Ralph, this boy could be your twin! Are you two related?'

'No,' hissed Ralph, holding out a protective hand. 'Keep away, Myrtle. Your life is in danger.'

'Now, Ralph!' mocked the Doppelgänger. 'That's hardly fair. I mean we're so very closely related, to insult me is to insult yourself.'

He turned to Myrtle, took a bow and then, faster than Ralph could have thought possible, he lashed out. He hit Myrtle so hard that she lifted into the air and landed some ten feet away in a snowdrift. She lay unmoving.

'What the hell!' exclaimed Ralph and started to go to her, but the Doppelgänger grabbed him and stopped him. Ralph's haversack fell off his shoulder and landed on the road.

'Why are you doing this?'

The Doppelgänger held him in a grip of iron.

'So, Ralph,' he said, 'how does it feel to have nowhere to go? To be on the run, to be accused of murder, to know that you're going to hang?'

Ralph, rendered powerless by the Doppelgänger's strength, managed to gasp.

'I thought you would know. You are me after all, aren't you?'

He looked over at Myrtle. She moaned and moved slightly. Something protective stirred in Ralph.

The Doppelgänger, no doubt by design, was holding Ralph by his bad arm. The pain was excruciating. Mr Doran's dying face swam in front of his eyes and Ralph heard the old man's voice again.

'Kill it, boy, stab it through the heart.'

He still had the dagger in his free hand, concealed in the fold of his coat. He tightened his hold on the handle and imagined what it would feel like to plunge it into this evil creature. But how could he stab this person who looked so much like himself? What would happen? Then out of nowhere he was struck by an appalling thought,

How do I know I won't kill myself?

The Doppelgänger laughed. And Ralph was strangely unnerved to hear it. For just one moment he thought that he himself had laughed.

'I know what you're thinking,' said his black-hearted enemy. '"If I kill him, will I kill myself?" A good question. But you ain't got the guts to kill me yet, I can tell. I could kill you though, right now, just by wringing your scrawny neck. But where's the fun in that?'

He twisted Ralph's arm harder, causing him to shout out. Ralph grimaced.

'Fun? Is this just some sort of game for you? You killed Mr Doran because of a game?'

The Doppelgänger shrugged coldly, as if he didn't understand the question.

'Of course. Why not? Poor old Doran, he should have known better. Besides, he didn't play fair. Oh, and you're the loser in this game, in case you didn't know. What did the old man tell you, "Kill it or be killed"? I can see from your face that I'm right. Take my advice, don't even bother trying. Just give up now. How can you possibly expect to win against me? I have all the advantages. I know you inside out.'

Ralph felt anger rising in his guts.

'Mr Doran warned me you would say that. Don't forget, I know you too.'

The Doppelgänger's face changed, as if one mask had been taken off to reveal another beneath.

'Then you should know not to threaten me, Ralph. This is your only chance. Surrender now or die.'

'And if I surrender what will happen?'

The Doppelgänger twisted his mouth into a sneer.

'If you surrender, then I will kill you quickly. You see, I am not entirely without mercy. We do have something in common, though I would never snivel as you do.'

Ralph gritted his teeth and shook his head. The Doppelgänger's harsh laugh rang in his ears.

Do I really sound like that?

'Don't be a fool, Ralph. Make it easy on yourself. Surrender and die quickly, painlessly even; or fight and die a slow, excruciating death. These are my terms.'

Ralph was repulsed by the pure malice that burned in the eyes of the Doppelgänger. Worst of all, Ralph was looking into his own eyes. He was both shocked and repulsed.

Could that be me? Could I be that evil?

A chill of despair was creeping through him, but he fought it. If he surrendered now, he'd be giving up on Myrtle too. He spoke slowly, deliberately.

'It seems to me the outcome is the same whatever I choose. I will not surrender.'

The Doppelgänger threw Ralph roughly to the ground.

'Then go,' he snarled, giving him a vicious kick in the leg. 'Run for your life. What are you waiting for?'

Ralph looked over at Myrtle. She was trying to sit up. He got to his feet and stumbled across to her, taking her by the hand.

'Ah,' said the Doppelgänger from right behind him. 'How sweet.' He placed his foot squarely in Ralph's back and shoved him face down into the snow.

'Don't worry about the girl. Look out for yourself for once in your miserable life. If you're going to fight, at least put up a decent one. Think of me as Mrs Harbledown. What would you like to do to her if you got the chance?'

Ralph, on his knees, slush dripping down his chin, looked from Myrtle to the Doppelgänger and back again. He felt sick to the core.

I can't leave her, I can't.

'Uhnnh!' he grunted as he tried to get up.

The Doppelgänger had kicked him again, but this time the blow was followed by another and another. Trying to protect himself Ralph scrambled away on his hands and knees, all the time under attack. He began to sob.

He's going to kill me!

Finally the Doppelgänger let up just long enough for him to stagger to his feet and run. He looked back only once and Myrtle's pleading eyes watched him go. The Doppelgänger was standing in the middle of the road, a twisted smile playing about his mouth.

Ralph was normally a good runner, but now he was hampered by the snow and ice and also by injury. The Doppelgänger had kicked him so hard that every time his foot touched the ground an agonising pain shot up his leg. Behind him, he could hear the steady pounding of the Doppelgänger's feet. He was running too, but easily. The head start he had allowed Ralph was almost gone and the gap between them was closing fast.

Spurred on by sheer dread, Ralph kept going but his pace was decreasing and the pursuing footsteps were getting louder and louder. Now he could hear breathing – harsh, laboured, breathing. But not the Doppelgänger's. The monster had hardly broken a sweat.

That's my breathing! he realised.

Ralph's chest was burning from the cold and the effort of running over the slippery terrain and his injured leg was leaving an uneven trail in the snow.

'You can't get away from me, Ralph,' called the Doppelgänger effortlessly. 'Think about it. You're just running away from yourself. I'll get you. I can already touch you.'

To his horror, Ralph felt something grazing his back. He looked over his shoulder and there was the Doppelgänger, merely an arm's reach away. His own arm's reach! The monster's face was so contorted with malice that it barely looked like him anymore. All the time he was laughing like a maniac. Ralph saw his hand reaching out for him, a grasping claw, and he felt a fear he had never experienced before. He took a huge painful breath and with one monumental effort he sprinted out of reach of his terrible pursuer.

At the limits of his endurance, Ralph ran on blindly and suddenly found himself in Salter's Alley. Up ahead he saw the sign for the Smuggler's End. He let out a choking moan as he realised the terrible danger he was heading towards. On the verge of complete collapse, gasping for every breath, he stumbled past the tavern. As he entered the town square he ran full pelt into the arms of a stranger, and he clung for his life to the man's coat.

'Hell's teeth!' exclaimed a gruff voice. 'You're that boy they're all looking for, from Harbledown's tavern!'

Ralph looked up into the scowling face of a city constable.

Incapable of speech, fighting for every breath, Ralph didn't even try to escape the constable's grip. The constable, now holding Ralph in an armlock, reached into his pocket and took out his whistle. He blew an ear-splitting blast that echoed around the empty streets. Almost immediately, in response to the whistle, two men appeared and ran towards them. Both were wearing the unmistakeable top hat and blue coat of the town constables. Ralph's captor called them over.

'Ere! Look what I got, the boy from the Smuggler's End! I caught the little blighter!'

Out of the corner of his eye Ralph saw the Doppelgänger's smirking face poke around the corner. He gave a sinister wink and was gone.

'You're choking me!' Ralph managed to croak. He felt the grip around his throat loosen a tad.

'Get used to it, lad,' laughed the constable. 'You'll be choking in the noose soon enough. And until then, we've got a nice little room for you down at the station, somewhere you can think over your foul deed before you pay for it. Killing a defenceless old man, have you no shame?'

He took out a pair of rusty handcuffs, fastened them around Ralph's wrists and began to drag him down the road.

Chapter Eight

Ralph sat in his cell, his cuffed hands resting on his knees. He shivered. His feet were so cold he could no longer feel them and he was aching all over. The fire in his lungs was finally easing. The tiny space was filthy and stank to high heaven. The only natural light and air came in through a barred, unglazed window set high up in the wall. He was utterly exhausted but didn't dare to close his eyes. He was too afraid of what might happen while he slept.

Not that I could get any sleep, he thought miserably. *The racket in this place would make sure of that.*

The putrid air was filled by a horrible chorus of groaning, wailing, coughing and rattling. Ralph went to the door and looked out. There were cells to the left and right. The jailer was a mountain of a man who was as wide as he was tall. Every so often he thundered along between the cells and dragged one of the inmates away. Ralph knew his turn would come before too long.

And then what? he wondered. *Prison or straight to the gallows?*

Ralph felt as bruised and battered as if he had been in a bare-knuckle boxing fight. How could things have possibly turned out this way? Even his attic room at the Smuggler's End was paradise compared to this.

He fought back tears of frustration and self-pity.

'I should have known not to try,' he whispered. 'When has anything ever worked out for me? Fingers was right – I am a useless, snivelling coward.'

He let out a groan when he remembered Myrtle. He had left her in the snow. He would never forget that look in her eyes. He had betrayed her friendship. It sickened him to think that the Doppelgänger might be right, that they had something in common.

Because I am him and he is me, thought Ralph.

Voices and the sound of metal against metal jolted him out of his misery. He steeled himself for what was to come.

'Ralph Bennett?' the jailer called out.

'Here,' he mumbled. All his courage had vanished, like dust on the wind.

'You have a visitor.'

A visitor? His heart leapt. Someone to help him out of this fix? Myrtle! But why would she help? He had left her to die in the snow. He watched anxiously as the visitor walked down the dark corridor towards his cell. He could tell it wasn't Fingers or Mrs Harbledown, but neither was it Myrtle. As the person drew nearer Ralph crinkled his face in confusion. No! Surely it couldn't be …

'Hello, Ralph,' said the boy, pulling off his hat. 'Don't look so surprised. I thought you'd be expecting me.'

Through the bars Ralph stared once again into his Doppelgänger's evil face. With each encounter, Ralph was less and less sure that there were any differences between them at all.

'You again,' said Ralph, praying that his terror was not obvious. 'Now what do you want?'

'Just to see how you're doing.'

The Doppelgänger looked around.

'Hmm, it's not so nice in here. But don't worry, I doubt it'll be for long. They deal with murder cases quickly, especially at night. It's Judge Rightmire. You know, the fellow they call "The Noose".'

Ralph did know. The whole town knew. Judge Rightmire wasn't called The Noose for nothing. He had a reputation for dealing out swift justice, which more often than not involved hanging.

'It's you who should be before the judge,' said Ralph bitterly. 'I don't know why you think you can get away with this. How can you, you look like me!'

A smile played at the corners of the Doppelgänger's mouth.

'Oh, I don't worry about things like that. Once you're er … gone, I can change how I look. It doesn't take much, a bit of hair dye'll do the trick. And, of course, I'll get out of these rags. It's amazing how little notice people take of what is right in front of them. They'll soon forget you, anyway. You're nothing special. There's a murder every day in this town. And I won't be sticking around here. As soon as you're finished, I'll be off.'

'Why are you doing this to me?' Ralph said, wondering whether it was it even possible to reason with this … this creature.

The Doppelgänger let out a sigh of forbearing.

'Oh, Ralph, you really don't get it do you? The whole point of my existence is to kill you. We cannot possibly both exist. It is against the laws of nature. We need to be as one.'

'Laws of nature? What's nature got to do with this? You're just a cold-blooded killer!'

To Ralph's disbelief, the Doppelgänger actually looked hurt.

'That's hardly fair! Dear me! I have some explaining to do. You see, I'm not really killing you, I'm becoming you. Or the other way around if you prefer it. Can't you feel the connection between us? I'm just another part of you. You will live on in me. Together we will make a properly whole person. Have you never thought that there was something missing from your life? I'm the part you keep hidden, the thoughts you don't voice, the impulses you quash. Don't you see? Without me you are only half a person. With me, you will be complete.'

Ralph nearly laughed out loud.

'I'm complete as I am. I don't need you. I've done very well without you.'

'Have you? How long have you put up with Ena Harbledown's taunts and savagery? You should have sorted her out years ago.'

'But I couldn't,' protested Ralph weakly. 'I had nowhere to go, no money, and Fingers would have come after me. I'm not a thief or a murderer. I'm not you.'

The Doppelgänger came closer to the bars and lowered his voice.

'Exactly. Now let's stop kidding ourselves, shall we? How often have you lain in bed at night and wanted to put your hands around old Ena's throat and squeeze the life out of her? What stopped you, Ralph?'

Ralph clenched his fists. How many times had he asked himself the same question?

'Maybe I thought it, but I didn't do it because it's wrong.'

The Doppelgänger chuckled, as if he had heard a joke.

'Wrong? Who says? There's no right or wrong, there's only surviving or dying. Life's what you make it, Ralph. You didn't ask to be born poor; it was bad luck. You could have been born rich in one of those fancy houses. Get what you want Ralph, don't hold back. You only have one life. The universe doesn't care about right or wrong. We're nothing to it. Mere specks of dust.'

Ralph knew what the Doppelgänger was saying shouldn't make sense, so how come some of it did? '

I know what you're doing. Mr Doran said you would try to confuse me.'

'Hah,' snorted the Doppelgänger. 'Doran? That old fool. Forget about him. Think, Ralph, what we could do together. I'm everything you're not. That's the beauty of it. You know I wouldn't have put up with that old witch. I'd have done her in a long time ago and taken her money. You've earned it, don't you think? You don't have the guts to do what needs to be done.

You're weak, Ralph. With me you won't be.'

'But Mr Doran killed his Doppelgänger. So I can kill you.'

Ralph heard the words that were passing his lips, but he knew that he didn't really believe them. And the Doppelgänger knew it too. How could he possibly kill anyone, or anything, from inside a prison?

Swiftly the Doppelgänger came right up to the bars and reached between them, beckoning with his pale hands. His voice was soothing now, oozing like grease from a cooked goose.

'Come here, Ralph. Let me put you out of your misery. It'll be quick, I promise you. Quicker than the noose. Sometimes they don't die straightaway you know, they just suffocate slowly. I'll be doing you a favour. This way your life won't be wasted. You'll feel everything as before but you will be stronger, more confident. Dammit, Ralph, I can even make you rich!'

Ralph was utterly drained in mind and body. Hardly knowing what he was doing, he began to move towards the beckoning hands of the Doppelgänger. It was like wading through water. All the time his fatigued mind was thinking.

Maybe the Doppelgänger is right. What chance do I have now really? I'm going to be hanged for murder. A murder I didn't commit. All my life I have been afraid and now here is an opportunity to never be afraid again. Why not take it? What difference will it make in the end? I'm dead either way. The Doppelgänger isn't my enemy, he's my friend.

The Doppelgänger reached further in and Ralph gasped at the cold touch of the fingers on his neck. He closed his eyes. The Doppelgänger's hands tightened,

tightened around his throat. He was struggling to breathe. His knees were weakening. His head was spinning. Soon it would all be over.

'Ralph, you really are pathetic,' sneered the Doppelgänger, pushing him away. Ralph fell backwards onto the cold floor.

'I don't know why that girl ever had anything to do with you.'

Ralph got up, dazed and coughing.

'Myrtle? Is she still … is she dead?'

'What do you think? You left her to save yourself.' The Doppelgänger looked at him in disgust. 'Ralph, Ralph, you disappoint me. Would you really give up your life so easily? You know, I'm almost ashamed that we are connected. I'm tempted to let you hang.' He tipped his hat in farewell. 'I'll be seeing you.'

Ralph grabbed the bars and pressed his face up against them.

'I'll kill you, you devil!' he shouted.

'That's the spirit,' called back the Doppelgänger before disappearing into the dark with a chuckle.

Ralph threw himself down on the floor and howled.

Ralph was woken suddenly by a high-pitched screech. He stayed where he was, face down on the floor. He didn't know how long he had been asleep but it was dark outside. He was numb with cold and hopelessness.

'Ralph!' hissed a voice through the bars.

'Who is it?' He didn't even look up.

'It's me, Fingers.'

Ralph sat bolt upright. He had never thought that the sight of Fingers would gladden his heart. There behind him was Mrs Harbledown. He jumped off the bed and ran over to the bars.

'At last! Get me out of here. It's all been a terrible mistake. Did you see him? He was here. The murderer.'

'Didn't see no one,' said Fingers dismissively. 'They're taking you up any minute. Where's the gold? I'll tell the judge it weren't you if you give us a share.'

'But I don't have any gold,' insisted Ralph, exasperated. 'The box was empty.'

Fingers raised his eyebrows in disbelief.

'All right, then where's the box? That's got to be worth a bit. I mean to kill a man …'

'I didn't kill anyone! Just get me out of here.'

Mrs Harbledown snorted, as was her habit, like the pigs she favoured.

'I told you,' she said. 'We're wasting our time.' She began to walk away.

'No! Don't go, help me,' pleaded Ralph. 'You know I didn't do it.'

'I don't know nothin' of the sort,' said Mrs Harbledown.

'I'll tell them everything. About the knife-grinder … and the others.'

Ralph was ashamed of the desperation in his voice.

'Too late,' said Mrs Harbledown. 'We've told them already.'

'Stand away from the door,' growled a voice. 'Stand away.'

It was the jailer.

Chapter Nine

Ralph did as he was told. He had seen what happened to those who defied this huge man. He didn't carry that thick baton for nothing. The door opened and he was hauled roughly out of the cell and along the corridor.

'Where are you taking me?'

'You'll find out soon enough.'

They passed through two more barred iron doors and along a hallway which led to a set of steps. The jailer shoved Ralph ahead of him up the stairs. As he approached the top he realised that there was a trapdoor above him. The jailer rapped on the trapdoor with his baton and it was opened. With one final push Ralph found himself catapulted into a large, wood-panelled room. He squinted at the light. It wasn't that it was very bright, more that he had been sitting in the gloom for so long that the sudden contrast hurt his eyes. The trapdoor slammed shut behind him and Ralph felt another pair of hands guiding him forward. By the time his eyes had adjusted to the light he found he had been locked inside a cage.

So this was what a courtroom looked like.

Ralph stood and faced Judge Rightmire, a stern-faced man with bushy eyebrows and a deeply furrowed brow above a swollen red nose. The gallery around the courtroom was packed to the railings with hecklers and vagrants who came in for the warmth and entertainment.

'Name!', barked a tall, grey-suited man standing to the left of the cage.

'Ralph Bennett.'

'What are the charges, Mr Dunfor?' asked the judge, addressing the man in grey.

'Murder, your honour.'

'No,' protested Ralph quickly. 'It's a mistake. I haven't murdered anyone.'

Mr Dunfor shot him a sharp look.

'Speak only when you are spoken to,' he warned, 'or you'll be held in contempt.'

Ralph wasn't sure what that meant. Couldn't he defend himself?

Mr Dunfor turned back to the judge.

'This boy has been accused of the murder of a Mr A. P. Doran, a lodger at the Smuggler's End, a tavern of good repute owned by Mrs Ena Harbledown. It's a clear-cut case. We have the murder weapon taken from the accused upon capture.' He paused to hold up the dagger. 'And we have witnesses.'

'Bring them in,' said the judge, making no effort to stifle a huge yawn that reeked of whisky.

'What witnesses?' asked Ralph urgently. 'How can there be witnesses to a crime I didn't commit?'

'Silence!' thundered the judge, bringing down his gavel with a sharp thwack. 'You're in enough trouble as it is. Don't make it worse for yourself.'

Approaching footsteps heralded the arrival of the witnesses. Ralph looked up to see Mrs Harbledown and Fingers. This did not bode well at all.

Ralph recognised the look on Mrs Harbledown's face. It was the same expression she wore when the slaughterman came to collect the pigs – a look of gluttonous enjoyment. Fingers, hardly able to contain his excitement, was hopping from one foot to the other, rubbing his dirty hands together.

'Ena Harbledown, can you confirm that this boy before you is Ralph Bennett?'

'Oh, your honour, I'm ashamed to say it, but he is indeed Ralph Bennett. He looks after my pigs and works in the tavern. I always knew he wasn't to be trusted. Since the day I took him on, I could tell there was bad blood in his veins. I could see it in his face. That's what you get for charity.'

'Char—' began Ralph but stopped himself. How dare the woman claim to have looked after him! She had taken everything from him and now she was in the act of hammering the final nail into his coffin.

'Always complaining,' continued Mrs Harbledown. 'About his wages, about the drinkers, about the smell. He made false promises and skived off hard work. Looking for easy money, no doubt. And two other lodgers have gone missing, right under my nose.'

'Are you saying the boy has murdered before?' asked Mr Dunfor.

'Oh, oh,' wailed Mrs Harbledown, clasping her pudgy hands together and shaking her head. Ralph was astonished to see a tear roll down her cheek. 'It's the only explanation! If only I had taken more notice of what the boy was up to, those others would still be alive today.'

'The two-faced witch!' muttered Ralph. 'She's lying through her rotten teeth.'

Mrs Harbledown hadn't finished.

'That Mr Doran, the fella he murdered, he had a box of gold with him and now it's gone. The boy must've stole it. I'm lucky he didn't take the knife to me in my bed! To think he was living under my roof.'

'Thank you, Mrs Harbledown,' said Mr Dunfor. 'Call the next witness.'

Mrs Harbledown was led away weeping noisily as Fingers came eagerly up to the front of the court.

'I saw him do it,' he said, even before he was asked. 'He stabbed Mr Doran. Lord knows, I'll never forget it. It'll stay with me until the day I die. He was standing over that poor man with a dagger in his hand. And the blood in the room, like a river.'

'You dirty rotten liar!' shouted Ralph, unable to control himself any longer. He was shaking with fury at the sheer injustice of it all. 'You weren't even there!' He looked at Judge Rightmire. 'It wasn't me! They're the murderers, those two, I swear!'

The judge began to hammer with his gavel again, and one of the court constables rapped on the cage with his truncheon, but Ralph shouted above the noise at Fingers.

'Tell them the truth. It was another boy killed Doran. He even looks like me.'

The judge held the gavel in mid-air and laughed.

'Aye, aye,' he said. 'Not another case of mistaken identity! In my experience, the louder the denials, the likelier the guilt.'

Suddenly a shiver ran down Ralph's spine and dread surged through him. A movement in the gallery caught his eye and his pounding heart skipped a beat. For there, leaning calmly on the balcony, a broad grin across his face, was the Doppelgänger. He winked knowingly at Ralph.

'Look! That's him, up there! That's the boy you want.'

'Silence!' ordered Rightmire. 'You seem confused, boy, as to exactly who the murderer is. You cannot blame everyone in the courtroom. Why, you'll be pointing at me next!'

'Dammit, but it's him!' insisted Ralph.

Why would no one listen to him? All eyes turned to the gallery but it was too late. The Doppelgänger was already gone.

Ralph saw the judge's lips moving, he heard the words he was saying, but he couldn't take them in. Everything he knew, his very existence, was slipping away from him.

He looked at the grinning Fingers and at Mrs Harbledown drying her fake tears. He looked at Judge Rightmire and at Mr Dunfor. These people were bringing about his end and he could do nothing about it. Suddenly everything was clear. The Doppelgänger was right.

'I am but a speck of dust,' he whispered.

'… Ralph Bennett, I declare you guilty of murder. Tomorrow morning you are to be hanged by the neck until you are dead. Take him away.'

The cage door was opened and, in a daze, Ralph was dragged away through a back door to a reinforced prison wagon that was waiting in the yard. He was thrown inside, the door was slammed shut, and the bolts were locked with a loud clang.

Ralph staggered to his feet, his balance impeded by the fact that his hands were in cuffs. The wagon rocked from side to side as a constable clambered on to sit next to the driver. Ralph looked out of the narrow window and suddenly Fingers' face appeared in front of him.

'Last chance, lad,' he whispered. 'Tell us where you hid it.'

But before Ralph could say a word there was the sharp sound of a cracking whip, the wagon jerked forward and Fingers was gone. The horses' hooves crunched in the icy snow and they made off down the treacherous hill towards the prison.

As the wagon skidded and swerved on the icy road, Ralph was thrown from side to side. He tried to hold on to something but the cuffs made it practically impossible. Finally he managed to grab one of the metal hinges, bracing himself against the cold, metal doors. Was there no end to this nightmare? Was there no justice in the world?

'Not in Rightmire's courtroom,' he muttered. But then, did he really deserve mercy? Hadn't he abandoned Myrtle when she was at her weakest? It was the sort of thing Fingers would do or Mrs Harbledown. If he ever saw Myrtle again, he would make it up to her somehow, he vowed silently. He thought bitterly of how Mrs Harbledown and Fingers had turned against him.

When I get out of this mess, I swear my revenge will be worse than they could ever imagine.

But how was he going to get out of this mess? There was no chance to prove his innocence now. His only hope was to escape. He examined the cuffs in the moonlight that filtered through the window bars, but he could tell straightaway that they were not going to come off without a miracle. He could hear the constable and the driver up front laughing and joking. The prison wasn't far – down the hill and over the bridge. He was running out of time.

Suddenly there was an angry shout from the driver.

'Hey!'

Ralph crept to one of the slit windows and looked out.

'What the —!' he exclaimed, hardly able to believe what he was seeing. Standing in the middle of the road, right in the path of the horses, a figure was lit by the eerie blue light of a street lantern. Legs planted wide and hands on hips, it was the Doppelgänger.

'Get out of the way!' roared the driver.

The boy didn't move. The driver pulled hard on the reins, but the road was too slippery and the horses stumbled and panicked. The wagon skewed sideways, juddered, shook and bounced about the road. Ralph was thrown to the floor and tossed about like a stone in a jar. There was a terrible crashing sound as the wagon tipped over to come down heavily on its left side. It began to slide, and the sound of the metal scraping across the snow and ice and the rocky road underneath was like nails scraping down a blackboard. He reached out desperately with his cuffed hands to brace himself.

Still sliding, the wagon gained speed until it hit something solid and launched into the air. It was airborne for only a second or two before landing with a terrible impact and a huge splash.

We're in the river! thought Ralph before he slammed headfirst into the bench.

Stars clustered in front of his eyes and the last thing he saw was the side of the wagon bursting open.

Chapter Ten

For the second time in as many days, Ralph woke up to find himself lying flat on his back, unsure about what had happened. This time, however, there was no fire to warm him. He was shivering violently and the back of his head was throbbing with pain. He could see his breath in front of his face. He sat up groggily and blinked hard in the bright white light. Everything seemed the wrong way around. The wagon door was at an angle and he was sitting on a window. Water slopped in through the bars and ran down towards the door. And there was a huge hole in the side of the wagon, which was now almost above him. It took a few seconds for him to realise that the white light was from the moonlit snow on the river bank.

He managed to step up onto the bench and poke his head awkwardly out of the hole, trying to avoid the sharp and ragged edges of metal. The vehicle had landed in the shallows near the river bank. He looked all around. There was no other life to be seen, so he climbed painfully and awkwardly out of the hole in the wagon. He waded to the edge of the freezing water and crawled up the rocky bank to the top, where he paused to catch his breath. The wagon was quite a spectacle: a mangled wreck, lying awkwardly in the water, two wheels slowly spinning and two lost forever. The horses were standing huddled together by a tree and Ralph was strangely pleased to see that they had survived the accident.

He was equally pleased to find that, apart from the alarming lump on the back of his head, he seemed to have escaped serious harm. He enjoyed a few moments of confused but blissful ignorance before, in a sudden rush, the events of the previous few hours came back to him. He let out a loud groan and felt his heart sink. He had survived the crash but what horror now lay in store?

Aware that he was out in the open, he limped for cover behind a nearby tree. He peeked out and scanned the landscape. The full moon cast an eerie light across the snowy ground, not strong enough to show detail, only shapes. Ralph stared hard at a dark mound in the snow at the water's edge. It looked oddly out of place.

As certain as he could be that there was no one else around, Ralph made his way down to the water towards the strange mound. When he was only a foot or two away his fears were confirmed – it was the body of the constable from the wagon. He was face down in the snow and he was not breathing. There was no sign of the driver. Quickly Ralph knelt beside the dead man and pulled him over. This was no easy task considering his injuries and exhaustion, and the fact that the constable was evidently a well-fed man. He unbuttoned the dead man's coat.

'Yes!' he blurted with delighted relief when he saw the set of keys hanging on the constable's belt. He pulled them off and after a couple of attempts managed to unlock the handcuffs and toss them aside. Then he wrestled off the constable's heavy coat and put it on. It was much too big.

'Sorry,' Ralph whispered. 'But I need this much more than you.'

He checked in the pockets and was very pleased to find half of a baked potato, still warm, and a small flask of brandy. He took a gulp and felt the liquid blaze a burning trail down the back of his throat. He was beginning to feel better.

'Right,' he told himself. 'This is your last chance to get away. No more mistakes!'

Then he remembered Myrtle. Should he go back and look for her? He had not forgotten that only minutes ago he had vowed to make it up to her. But now, out in the open again, he wasn't so sure. He was almost certain that he had condemned her to death by leaving her at the mercy of the Doppelgänger. If he went back he was only putting himself in danger again.

But what if she's not dead?

Ralph dismissed the thought quickly. Something inside him had hardened and he couldn't take the risk. He pulled his new coat more closely about him and reached up to his shoulder. There was nothing there.

'My haversack!' he exclaimed. It had fallen off when the Doppelgänger had grabbed him outside the Spicy Fish. His sad and tired heart sank even lower. The haversack held all his possessions. Worst of all, it held the black box, and

Ralph didn't dare think what chaos might be unleashed if somebody else opened it. He had to recover it. He would have to go back.

Maybe I can help Myrtle after all …

Wearily he made his way over the river bank towards the bridge. He could see the blue glow of the gaslights further up the hill. He could also see the rock on the verge which had so dramatically launched the carriage into the air. There was a huge gouge in the road where the carriage had slid along. It was only then that Ralph remembered what had caused the accident. The Doppelgänger!

Fear, which had been simmering quietly, came quickly to the boil and churned violently in his stomach. He looked around uneasily. The Doppelgänger could be anywhere, watching him, plotting his next move. But the Doppelgänger was no longer his only problem. He saw lights and movement up ahead. A small crowd of people were hurrying down the road to the bridge, and at their head were more constables.

Ralph swore and slithered back down the slope to hide again in the wood. He watched from behind a tree as the people reached the bridge and began to clamber down the bank, sliding, tripping and cursing loudly. They were holding up powerful lanterns so he backed even further into the woods to avoid being seen.

'Check the wagon,' ordered a constable.

'It's empty,' shouted one man who had climbed onto it and looked inside.

'And here are the cuffs,' shouted another, holding up the open iron bracelet.

'The murdering wretch has escaped!' said the constable. 'He can't have gone far, look for footprints. We've got to get him, lads. Now he's responsible for the death of one of my men. He deserves to swing for that, not a doubt about it!'

'Great, just great,' muttered Ralph, looking at the very obvious line of footprints that led straight to where he was now hiding. He wasted no more time and took off swiftly into the trees. Immediately the cries of the men followed him.

'Hey! There's someone in the woods.'

'After him!'

They were out for his blood, and once again Ralph was running for his life. Normally he was sure he could outrun them. But he was exhausted. His injured leg hurt with every step and his bruised head was throbbing. He soon found that the constable's coat was so big it was holding him up, snagging on branches and bushes as he tried to get away. Finally it caught on a bramble bush and he had to shrug it off and leave it behind.

The further he went into the wood, the closer the trees were to each other and the harder it was to move forward. He looked anxiously over his shoulder. The lights were no nearer but neither were they any further away. The dark shadows behind the lanterns were like faceless monsters.

'I see 'im!' came a cry. 'Over there!'

'Keep going lads, we'll get 'im yet!' But strangely they were now heading in the wrong direction.

Ralph made for a gap between two trees. Too late, he saw a huge hollow in front of him. Solid ground disappeared from beneath his fleeing feet and he fell down the steep bank. He lay where he had landed, the breath knocked out of him, wheezing and gasping. He knew he should get up and keep going but when he tried to raise himself up he hadn't the strength any more. He fell back.

I can't go on, he thought. *I cannot win. If the constables don't get me, the Doppelgänger surely will.*

He closed his eyes, not feeling the cold. All he wanted now was to drift off into oblivion. He had accepted defeat and it was actually a relief to know that finally the struggle really was over.

Maybe I'll be lucky. Maybe I'll just wake up dead.

He licked his lips and tasted salt. His wandering mind was filled with lost opportunities. He could have sailed the seas and made his fortune in another land. He remembered what the Doppelgänger had said, about life and luck.

It's true, if I had been born into a different family, into money, then none of this would have happened.

But he had been born poor, to a mother who had died when he was barely walking and a cruel father who had sold him into the slavery of Mrs Harbledown for the price of a bottle of gin. The odds were stacked against him from his first breath.

'I never had a chance in hell,' he muttered. 'But at least I tried.'

A twig snapped nearby and there was a shuffling sound. He knew in his heart that the end had come. He could feel a presence and he heard the squeak of the snow as it was pressed down by feet right beside him. He didn't want to open his eyes. He just lay and waited for it to start.

'Hey!' hissed a voice. 'Get up, quick.'

'Just do it,' murmured Ralph through blue lips. 'Kill me, I surrender. I want to be you.'

'What? Hurry, they're nearly here.'

Ralph groaned and opened an eye. Someone was standing behind his head. He tilted his head back, fully expecting to see the cruel face of the Doppelgänger looking down at him. But this was not his wicked double bending over him. He squinted but couldn't make out the face. Then two arms reached down under his arms and began to tug. Unable to resist, in a state of exhausted confusion, Ralph allowed himself to be dragged backwards into a dark tunnel in the side of the hollow. Then he watched as his shadowy saviour dragged a thick branch across the entrance. What little light there had been was extinguished.

'Who —' he began, but instantly a hand clamped down hard over his mouth.

'Shhh, they're just outside.'

They sat unmoving, Ralph and his anonymous companion, and listened to the voices of the men outside. They were no more than a yard or so away.

'Where'd he go?'

'Blighter's disappeared. I think he's injured. Did you see how he was running?'

'There'll be a big reward. Rightmire doesn't like it when they escape. We'll probably find him tomorrow, half-frozen. Either that or he'll be here all winter and his bones'll surface when the snow melts.'

'I'd still like to see a noose around his neck.'

'Let's go. We've got to get the wagon out of the river.'

Presently the silence of the winter's night returned to the wood. The hand over Ralph's mouth was taken away. He heard a swooshing noise and saw the flare of a match being struck close to his ear. A pale face appeared only inches from his own. It was a little bloodied and bruised but there was no doubting who it was. He let out a cry of delight.

'Myrtle, are you all right?'

Chapter Eleven

'I'm so sorry,' blurted out Ralph immediately, now that it was safe to talk. 'For leaving you there with that monster. That was some whack he gave you.'

Myrtle smiled.

'You can say that again,' she joked. 'I wasn't out for long. I'm tougher than you think. It probably looked worse than it was. To be honest, you don't look so good yourself.'

Ralph marvelled at her good humour and strength. It was in stark contrast to his own shamefully downbeat attitude. Myrtle didn't look strong at all – in fact she looked very underfed. He put his hand up to his bruised head.

'How on earth did you find me? I mean, why did you even bother to come looking for me?'

Myrtle shrugged.

'Why wouldn't I? You needed help. I couldn't just leave you.'

Ralph went red and turned his head away from the light.

'Even after I left you?'

'You didn't have much of a choice,' she said matter-of-factly.

'Perhaps,' whispered Ralph.

'Anyway, by the time I managed to get up you were both gone. I followed the tracks in the snow and got as far as the town square, near the Smuggler's End, but then there were so many footprints in the road that I had to stop. I even thought to knock at the tavern to see if you were there.'

Ralph interrupted with a very loud snort.

'But then,' Myrtle continued, 'I saw Fingers and Mrs Harbledown rushing off towards the police station. I knew then that you'd end up at the court. I was up in the gallery. I watched the whole show but you didn't see me.'

'But you saw the Doppelgänger?'

Myrtle frowned.

'Doppelgänger? What sort of name is that?'

'I mean the boy, the one who looks like me.'

'Oh, yes, but only for a second. As soon as you pointed him out, he disappeared. Anyway, I followed the prison wagon. I don't know what I thought I would do, I just wanted to help. I heard the wagon crash and when I saw it in the river I was sure that you were dead. I could hardly believe it when you climbed out. Then all those people came and started to chase you. And now here you are.'

'Was it you I heard sending them off in the wrong direction?'

'Yes, it gave me just enough time to get to you. But I don't understand what you were doing lying in the snow. What were you talking about?'

Ralph reddened.

'I'd given up,' he said quietly. 'I just wanted to die. I thought you were that boy.'

Myrtle looked shocked. 'But you must never give up,' she insisted. 'If you give up, then it's all over. That's what my grandfather used to say.'

Obviously determination ran in the family, thought Ralph.

'That's all very well, but as far as I can see I'm dead either way.'

Myrtle tutted.

'Oh my, Ralph, if I'd known you were so weak I wouldn't have saved you. You said you wanted to get on a ship. So, that's what you must do. Sail away to where no one knows you.' She hesitated. 'You know, I'd like to come along too. The tales the sailors tell of other lands where it's warm all the time, you should hear them. And there's nothing here for me. My uncle is dead, I have no other family.'

'Why not!' replied Ralph, immediately feeling happier.

Myrtle smiled. 'Great! Oh, and I almost forgot, I have something for you.'

She reached beside her and handed over Ralph's haversack.

'I thought I'd never see it again!' he exclaimed with delight.

He was suddenly very aware of how pathetic he had been.

'Thank you,' he said quietly. 'For everything, for saving me. Next time I won't leave you, I promise.'

'Be careful,' warned Myrtle with her already familiar grin. 'I might hold you to that. Now, follow me. Let's get out of the cold and to somewhere safer.'

The tunnel was just high enough for the two of them to stand up and Myrtle moved off quickly, holding the light out in front of her. Ralph followed her down the twisting passage. Not slowed down by injury and confident of the way, Myrtle kept up a steady pace. Ralph soon lost count of the turns he had taken. He could feel something running down the side of his face and when he touched it his fingers came away dark red. His head was bleeding.

'Where exactly are we?' he asked.

'Smugglers' caves,' called Myrtle over her shoulder. 'Been here for hundreds of years. They go for miles into the cliff, all the way down to the sea, and they're full of dead ends. Some tunnels are even in a figure-of-eight. I think they're my favourite.' She glanced back at Ralph and laughed. 'Don't look so worried. I know them like the back of my hand. Just stick with me.'

'I will,' he said. 'We're going to get to that ship. Whatever it takes.'

He was exhausted and aching, but he also felt hopeful, in a strange sort of way. He was amazed by Myrtle. Nothing seemed to worry her. And she was right – he was being weak. Mrs Harbledown had crushed his spirit for years. But no more.

Eventually the tunnel widened out into a small chamber. Myrtle hung the lantern on a hook on the rocky wall. Ralph could see that there were more tunnels leading away from the chamber in every direction. He breathed in loudly. He could smell salt in the air and looked around curiously. There were all the signs that someone lived here: clothes, a makeshift bed, food and a small fire burning in a rocky fireplace.

'Is this where you live?'

'Not bad, eh?' replied Myrtle poking the fire and throwing on another log. 'Though maybe not as good as a room at the Smuggler's End.'

Ralph laughed.

'Believe me, it's a hundred times better!' He sat with great relief on an old wooden chest right by the fire and held out his frozen hands. Almost immediately they began to tingle as the life came back into them. 'It's warmer than the tavern and I don't suppose you pay any rent.'

Myrtle laughed and sat opposite on a similar chest. Suddenly her face creased with concern.

'Your head's bleeding,' she said. She stood up and opened the chest, pulling out a piece of linen. 'Here, dab it with this.'

Ralph held the linen to his head until the blood finally began to cake. Myrtle took out some bread and a tin of tea and put a kettle on to boil.

'The smugglers used to meet here and plan their raids. One group would row out to whatever foreign ship was approaching, tie up the crew and steal the cargo. Then they'd come back to shore where their friends were waiting to offload the spoils.'

'And they brought it all here?' asked Ralph. 'But I thought it was sheer cliff all around these parts.'

'They used to haul it up using ropes and baskets, then load it onto pushcarts and wheel it through the tunnels. You can still smell the spices and tobacco on a warm day. And if any nosy customs officers found their way in, the lookouts would lead them deep into the cliff and leave them to die. If you didn't know your way you'd get lost and never be found. There's bones all over the place. Are you hungry? It's just bread and tea.'

Ralph nodded eagerly, taking the bread that Myrtle offered and the steaming mug of tea. He was beginning to feel alive again, but in a different way to before. For once, he thought he could feel a glimmer of hope.

'So, tell me, how do you know your way around?'

'My grandfather was a smuggler,' Myrtle replied easily. 'When I was younger he'd bring me down here and take me through the tunnels until I knew them as well as he did. Eventually he could blindfold me and I'd still find my way out. He's dead now, of course, and my mother and father. Father was hanged for smuggling.'

They ate in silence for a few minutes and then Myrtle wiped her mouth and brushed crumbs from her skirt.

'But that's enough about me. Tell me more about that boy and the murder. He's the one they should be after, isn't he?'

'Do you believe me now, that I didn't kill Mr Doran?'

Myrtle looked thoughtful.

'I wasn't sure at first, but to be honest you didn't seem the sort to murder anyone. You're a bit, well, gentle. When you grabbed me at the Spicy Fish, I could tell you hadn't done that before.'

Ralph reddened but said nothing.

'And then when I saw Fingers in the courtroom I spotted my uncle's waistcoat under his coat. I heard what he said to you too, about the box, before the wagon took off. That's when I decided you were innocent.' Myrtle looked suddenly grim. 'My uncle and the … pigs, are you sure about that?'

Ralph nodded.

'As sure as I can be.'

Myrtle poked at the fire wordlessly and Ralph began to talk, to fill the silence.

'You're right about me. I've been a coward. But things have changed, I've changed. The problem is that the Dopp … that boy wants to kill me, and he'll just keep trying until he succeeds. I still want to get to a ship, but he's bound to find us.' He hesitated. 'I have to kill him, it's the only way to get rid of him. Otherwise he'll always be after me.'

Myrtle stiffened.

I've said too much. Now she's afraid of me. Ralph stood up and began to pace back and forth in front of the fire, a worried expression on his face.

'It's really difficult to explain. But I swear you can trust me. You mustn't be afraid of me. I'm not going to hurt you.'

Myrtle tilted her head to one side. Ralph couldn't tell what she was thinking. And she still had hold of the poker. When she spoke, she spoke quietly.

'I do trust you. Remember, I saw that boy, I heard what he said to you, I felt his fist. Wherever he came from, whoever he is, I can tell that he's a nasty piece of work. But all this talk of killing. Is it really necessary?'

'Believe me, it's me or him,' said Ralph. 'He caused the wagon to overturn. He didn't want me to die, not yet, just to be free so he could hunt me down. He enjoys the chase. It's all a game to him. Did you see where he went?'

Myrtle looked troubled.

'No, he disappeared after the crash. Too many people about for comfort, I reckon.'

'What if he followed us?'

Myrtle let out a burst of laughter.

'He'll never find his way. Only smugglers or their descendants know their way around these tunnels. Anyone in your family a smuggler?'

'Not as far as I know.'

'There you are, we're safe.'

'For now.' Unable to help it, Ralph yawned. 'I'm so tired. I could sleep for a month.'

'Then rest,' said Myrtle. 'I'll keep watch, just in case this boy turns up, though I'm sure he won't.'

Ralph pulled a shirt from his haversack to use as a pillow, dislodging the black box as he did so, sending it tumbling across the floor and landing on Myrtle's foot. The box let off a soft glow, and Myrtle's eyes locked on the box.

Ralph turned to look at Myrtle and lunged for the box.

'Don't touch it,' he warned. 'If I hadn't opened it, I wouldn't be in this mess.'

'What do you mean? It's just so beautiful!' Her eyes never left the box.

'I stole it from Mr Doran and that's when all the trouble started. Whatever you do, don't touch it.'

Ralph set the box next to his makeshift pillow, uneasily watching Myrtle stare at the box.

'Ouch! she said suddenly, dropping the poker and rubbing her hand where the red hot metal had burnt it.

'The box is trouble, see?' Ralph said. 'Are you ok?'

'I'm fine,' Myrtle replied, still staring at the box. 'It looks valuable. You could sell it.'

'I was going to.' He lay down, putting the box in the crook of his arm and closed his eyes.

'But now I'm not so sure.'

Moments later he was asleep. Myrtle, on the other hand, was wide awake. Oblivious to the angry red burn across her palm, she remained transfixed by the gleaming box, wondering at the mysterious glow that shone when the box touched her foot.

Chapter Twelve

Ralph woke. The fire was out and he felt cold. The lantern was sputtering as he sat up on one elbow.

'Myrtle?'

His voice echoed around the empty chamber. In a sudden panic he looked down. No, it was all right, the black box was there on the floor beside him. He got up and took the lantern from the hook, topped it up with oil and turned up the wick. Then, one by one, he shone it down the tunnels. They all looked the same. He couldn't even tell by which one they had come into the chamber. And he could see that further down each rocky corridor, just at the limit of the light's reach, there were still more dark entrances. But he could see no sign of Myrtle. Where had she gone? More importantly, why had she gone?

Ralph immediately thought the worst.

Maybe she doesn't trust me after all. Maybe she thinks I am the murderer. Maybe she's going to turn me in.

He could have kicked himself for being so naïve, for accepting so blindly the help of a stranger. He stared into the darkness and could feel that familiar sense of hopelessness creeping up on him.

'No,' he said fiercely. 'Mrs Harbledown can't get to me now. It's not over. Just stop and think. This doesn't make sense. Myrtle went out of her way to help me, to take me somewhere safe. Why would she betray me now?'

But he had not failed to notice that this 'place of safety' was so safe he could not find his way out.

It works both ways, he thought.

Ralph looked around the chamber. As far as he could see, everything was as it had been before.

Perhaps she's gone to get food.

It was quite cold now and he tried to revive the fire. However, there was no wood left so he decided to look for some while he waited for Myrtle's return. He picked up the black box and started off down one of the tunnels, armed with a piece of charcoal to mark the turns.

Not far from the chamber he found a rocky shelf at head height and wedged the box at the back where it sat completely out of sight. He would collect it later. Further on he came across of one of the smugglers' pushcarts. The dried wood looked perfect for burning. He gathered up an armful of the wood and two rusty wheel spokes.

'Could be useful,' he murmured, looking at the sharp ends.

He was about to return to the chamber when he felt a sudden gust of air. He breathed in deeply and noted a strong smell of salt and seaweed. It set him thinking.

If that's a sea breeze, maybe I can follow it and find my way to the shore. It might even be possible to get out of here. No harm knowing an escape route!

So he put down the wood and licked his finger to determine the direction of the breeze. Then, at every crossroads, he licked it again to choose the tunnel to take. Religiously, he marked the rocky wall with a number and an arrow, using the piece of charcoal he had taken from the fire.

His footsteps echoed through the rocky maze, sounding as if they could be coming from any direction. More than once Ralph looked over his shoulder to satisfy himself that there was no one there. And more than once he found himself back at a corner he had already marked.

Myrtle said some of the tunnels were in the shape of a figure of eight, he recalled.

Every so often he thought he inhaled the lingering smell of spices. But eventually, with the sea still nowhere in sight, Ralph began to wonder whether he should turn back. The charcoal was wearing away rapidly.

One more turn, he decided, *and then I'll go back*.

Having convinced himself that he was on a fool's trail, he was both shocked and delighted when he rounded the corner and saw light at the end of the tunnel.

'Never give up,' he murmured with a smile.

The breeze was much stronger now and as he went towards the light he could actually feel sea spray on his face. He licked his lips and tasted brine. He hurried up the slight incline to the tunnel's end and stopped sharply just in time. He was teetering on the edge of a sheer drop to the sea.

'Phew!' he exhaled taking a step back from the edge. He crawled to the ledge and peered out into the cold, fresh air. Dawn was approaching. The red sun, half hidden by purple clouds, was just rising on the horizon. The tide was out and directly below him Ralph could see a narrow strip of sand dotted with menacing, jagged rocks. Beyond that the grey sea stretched away. There was a clear channel between the rocks, just wide enough for a smuggler's boat.

It was then Ralph noticed the thick rope tied to a metal ring set into the wall beside him. It was connected to a pulley outside the tunnel in the cliff face. Ralph tugged on it and it moved slowly.

Myrtle said ropes were used by the smugglers for hauling up the spoils, he thought. It reached practically all the way down to the sand. *Well, if it came to it*, he mused, *I suppose I could use it to climb down.*

For now, however, unable to go any further he started back, following the charcoal marks in reverse. He came to the pile of wood and collected it up. As he drew nearer to the chamber he found the ledge with the black box. It was still there, untouched and intact. He set off again but he was stopped in his tracks by a hiss. He thought he had imagined it, but then he heard it again.

'Psst!'

His heart nearly froze. Was it his Doppelgänger? But how? As quietly as he could he put down the wood, keeping one long piece as a makeshift weapon.

'Ralph, is that you?'

'Myrtle!' he hissed back. 'You nearly gave me a heart attack! Where are you?'

'In here.'

He traced the voice to a low tunnel to his left and shone in the lantern. Myrtle was about half way down, just out of sight around a bend, lying awkwardly on the ground. He let out a low exclamation and hurried towards her.

'Myrtle, what happened?' He helped her to sit up against the wall. She held her right arm tightly against her body and when he moved her leg, she stifled a cry of pain. Blood streaked her forehead and face and in the glow of his lantern she looked a deathly colour.

'Oh, Ralph,' she said and he thought she was about to burst into tears. 'I'm so sorry. It was that black box. You were asleep and I couldn't resist it. I only wanted to touch it, but as soon as I did, then I just had to know what was inside it. I used the key on the string around your neck. You were so fast asleep you didn't even move when I took it and unlocked the box.'

Ralph's eyes widened and he swallowed hard.

'What … what happened next?'

Myrtle groaned and rubbed her arm.

'I swear I don't know. As soon as the lid fell open I felt this force just come from nowhere and knock me over. Then another girl, just like me, appeared in the chamber and started to attack me. I couldn't do anything, she was so strong, and then she threw me against the wall. I must have passed out. When I woke up she was gone so I dragged myself here to hide. I think my arm is broken.' She looked up at Ralph, tears welling in her eyes. 'Is this something to do with that boy who's following you? Is this what you mean about the box causing all your trouble?'

'Oh no!' Ralph groaned. 'I should have told you.'

'Told me what?'

'You've set your Doppelgänger free.'

Ralph explained as quickly as he could, about Mr Doran and his Doppelgänger, even how he had almost let it strangle him in the cell.

'He said I would be better off dead.' It was a great relief to tell her the truth at last. 'I couldn't tell you before, you would have thought I was mad. Maybe you do now.'

Myrtle laughed weakly.

'You know, I've heard of Doppelgängers. Grandfather said the sailors used to see them at sea. They were omens of death. If a sailor saw his Doppelgänger he would just throw himself overboard there and then.'

Ralph shook his head.

'I don't know about at sea, but your Doppelgänger is somewhere in these tunnels. If she finds us she will certainly kill you, and most likely me too.'

Ralph knew he had to keep calm but panic was coming and going in waves, rising and falling in the pit of his stomach. He swallowed hard. His mouth had gone completely dry.

'What if your Doppelgänger's gone to get my Doppelgänger?'

Myrtle seemed more alert now, more like her old self.

'Let's not get carried away. We have to find the other Myrtle, let's call her Doppel Myrtle, before she finds us. I think you should go to the chamber to see if she is there. If she isn't, maybe we can get out that way.'

Ralph nodded. He felt nauseous with terror.

'Okay, but you wait here.'

'I'm not going anywhere.'

'I haven't forgotten my promise.'

Myrtle frowned quizzically.

'To not leave you again.'

'Oh, that. Well, needs must, Ralph.' Myrtle nodded towards the exit, urging him to go.

Ralph left Myrtle reluctantly and crept along the main tunnel towards the chamber. He could see an orange glow up ahead and his heart sank.

'Someone's there, they've lit the fire.'

He turned his lantern right down and left it on the ground. The last ten yards were the worst. His heart was like a blacksmith's hammer, thudding in his chest. He could feel sweat oozing out of his forehead. His chest had tightened so he could hardly breathe.

Flattening himself against the wall Ralph inched towards the chamber. He could see a shadow, Myrtle's shadow, *Doppel Myrtle* he reminded himself, moving to and fro in the room. Then all of a sudden another shadow appeared on the wall. It went up to Doppel Myrtle and, to Ralph's surprise, seemed to embrace her.

Slowly he began to shuffle away.

I might have had a chance against one, he thought, *but two?*

Chapter Thirteen

Back in the tunnel, Myrtle had moved to a more comfortable position in Ralph's absence. She looked up as he hurried towards her and her face creased in pain.

'She's in there all right,' he said, sitting beside her. He began to wipe at the blood on her face, but Myrtle stopped him.

'It's only a scratch.'

'Doppel Ralph is with her. I think they're working together. She must have gone to get him after she attacked you.'

'Of course,' said Myrtle. 'She's me, she knows her way around the tunnels.'

Ralph chewed on his lip. He hadn't thought of that.

'We need to make a plan, and quickly. We have to kill them both, that's what Mr Doran said, but they're very strong.'

'I know,' said Myrtle, holding up her injured arm. 'They've both had a go at me, remember.'

'It's not beyond us,' he said, steeling himself against the terror he felt. He didn't want her to see how scared he really was and how hopeless he believed their situation to be. 'We have to stab them through the heart.'

Myrtle snorted.

'We? Look at me Ralph. My arm is broken. And my ankle is twisted. I can't stand up. I can't walk. I can hardly stab someone.'

'Maybe we can get out of here without going through the chamber. I saw a rope on the cliff —'

Myrtle shook her head.

'We'd still need a boat. And I couldn't make it anyway.'

'But I could. And then I could come back, with weapons, and help you. My Doppelgänger doesn't know these tunnels, but I marked a trail.'

'Smart,' she said, then shook her head. 'It won't work. I mean, how would you get back to the chamber from the woods when you don't know the way?'

'I'll think of something,' he said desperately. 'Never give up, right?'

Myrtle looked at him oddly.

'Would you even come back?'

'Of course. I told you, I wouldn't leave you here.' He hoped she couldn't see how his cheeks burned; the awful truth was the thought had crossed his mind. 'They must be laughing right now,' he said bitterly. 'They've got us exactly where they want us. The thrill of the chase is as much what they're after as the final kill. They like to toy with their prey, before killing it. Like a cat with a mouse.'

'If only I hadn't opened the box,' said Myrtle quietly. 'This is all my fault.'

Ralph hadn't heard Myrtle sound regretful before. She was the one who had kept him going until now.

'Don't blame yourself, you couldn't help it, I should know! There's something about that box. It's impossible to resist. I know it looks bad but there has to be a way.'

Myrtle sighed.

'What did Mr Doran do? Did he say anything that might help?'

Ralph tried to think.

'He said to brand it, but I haven't had the chance. And he said he stabbed his Doppelgänger to death. "Kill it or become it", those were his last words.'

'Kill it or become it?' repeated Myrtle mournfully. 'Maybe we should just give up now. It's hopeless. We could become them, like your Doppel said when you were in the prison. Would it really be so bad? I mean, there's plenty about my life I want to change. If I was my Doppelgänger, then —'

Now it was Ralph's turn to be horrified.

'No,' he said firmly. 'I'm not going to let them win, and neither are you.' Secretly Ralph hoped he looked as confident as he sounded, because inside he was a mess. The tense silence was broken by a call which echoed down the tunnels.

'Oh, Ralph! Where are you? You'll get lost. Come back, I've cooked us up something. Do I have to come and get you?'

Myrtle looked at Ralph with wide and frightened eyes.

'It's Doppel Myrtle. She's trying to trick you into going back. What are we going to do?'

Ralph set his mouth in a firm line.

'I'm going to draw them into the tunnels one at a time and kill them both. That's what I'm going to do.'

An odd look crossed Myrtle's face, but it was gone before Ralph even registered it.

'But you don't have any weapons,' she protested.

'The constable took my dagger, but I've still got the spokes from the barrow wheels and they're sharp enough. Don't try to change my mind. It's the only way. You said it yourself, we can't let them come to us. We've got to go to them.'

'I didn't think you had it in you,' said Myrtle.

'Neither did I.'

And was that admiration in her eyes? Or something entirely different?

His nerves in shreds, Ralph left Myrtle's hiding place and stepped again into the main passageway. He was holding one spoke in his hand and the other was fixed to his belt. He set his lantern low. Cautiously he made his way to the chamber. Once more he watched the shadows. He could see that Doppel Myrtle was sitting up against the chest while Doppel Ralph was standing behind her. He was holding something, the poker? A dagger? It was difficult to tell.

Plotting our end, I bet. Well, two can play at that game. Ralph smiled a rather nasty smile and if he had seen himself in the mirror he might have wondered again how different he and his Doppelgänger really were.

With a shaking hand he picked up a stone and threw it into the chamber. Doppel Ralph turned sharply. Doppel Myrtle stayed where she was.

'Ralph? Is that you?'

She sounds different, there's a tremor in her voice – at the thought of killing me?

Doppel Ralph spoke.

'You might as well come out, Ralph. The game is drawing to a close. Accept it: this is the end for you. You know I will always find you. I know you too well.'

Ralph shifted his feet deliberately in the gravel.

Doppel Myrtle remained sitting, but Doppel Ralph laughed.

'I can hear you, Ralph. Why don't you come in and have something to eat? Think of it as a last supper.' He sniggered. 'If you don't, I'm coming after you. I'll count to ten. One …'

Time seemed to slow. Ralph gripped the spoke even tighter in his hand.

Come on, you two-faced wretch, he urged silently. *Come on.*

'Ten,' shouted the Doppelgänger. 'Here I come.'

Doppel Ralph moved quickly towards the entrance of the tunnel. Ralph ran off but not so fast that the Doppelgänger didn't see where he was going. He waited a second at each junction and crossways until he could be sure the Doppelgänger was coming and then, checking the marks on the wall, he headed off in the direction he had gone earlier.

Ralph knew he couldn't outrun the Doppelgänger, and he knew he couldn't beat him in a fist fight, but there was a possibility, a slight possibility, that he could outwit him. As he bounded through the tunnels, desperately trying not to skid on the gravelly, uneven floor, his mind was racing.

Odd, what Myrtle said, that she didn't think I had it in me. How many times have I heard that? Too many, but not from her. Strange what fear does to a person, I hadn't thought she was the sort to give up. I thought she was stronger than that. I'm the one who's supposed to be weak. But she is injured and I'm sure it's far worse than it looks. No wonder she's feeling hopeless.

He kept on running. Behind him the pursuing footsteps were gaining all the time.

At least I have an advantage; that creature has no idea where he's going.

But could he really see it through to the end?

I have to try. If I don't make it then Myrtle will suffer at the hands of those bloodthirsty beasts. Maybe I shouldn't have left her. Again … But what else could I do? She can't even walk. Surely it's better that one of us tries and fails, than for us both to give up and die? She wanted me to go.

The footsteps were closing in.

Just one more turn, then it'll all be over, one way or the other.

Ralph stopped at the final corner. He watched as the Doppelgänger came towards him. His face was contorted into a strange leer of triumph and menace. How could he ever have thought the two of them were alike?

'I've got you now, Ralph. Stand and fight, you coward. Have you no pride? No self-respect? Did you really think you could lose me in the tunnels? I can see your lamp, you fool.'

Ralph's heart was about to burst through his ribs but he didn't move.

Not yet! Not yet!

Now the Doppelgänger was so close he could actually smell him. Ralph watched as the monster reached out for him and then, in a sudden burst of speed, he ducked round the corner and sprinted towards the daylight. He reached the end of the tunnel in seven strides and jumped off the cliff and out into space.

The Doppelgänger, right on his heels, was unable to stop in time. With a cry he fell out and down onto the rocks below.

Chapter Fourteen

Ralph held on to the thick rope for dear life. He was swinging, in long arcs, back and forth across the cliff face, and at the same time descending. As he had so desperately hoped, the pulley held fast and slowed his descent. He looked down and could just make out in the dawn's early light the grossly deformed shape of the Doppelgänger lying spread-eagled on the rocks. Ralph could see that he was moving, and he could hear his groans. But still he fully expected to see the Doppelgänger get to his feet at any moment. At last, his own feet felt the firm sand and he let go of the rope.

But it wasn't over yet. Trembling from the chase and the superhuman effort of hanging on to the rope, Ralph went towards the moaning figure of the Doppelgänger. The tide was on the turn and small waves were beginning to lap around his body. He clambered between the rocks, which were as sharp as daggers, until he stood over the Doppelgänger. His head was badly disfigured, smashed in by the fall. There was blood running out of the corner of his mouth. He was hardly recognisable as Ralph.

But he was still alive.

Ralph looked straight into the dulling, soulless eyes.

'Very clever, Ralph, very clever,' gasped the Doppelgänger. 'You tricked me. But do you have it in you to finish the job? Then you can get back to your precious Myrtle.'

Silently revolted, Ralph patted down the Doppelgänger until he found what he was looking for: a dagger. He thought of Mrs Harbledown and the years of torture and abuse he had endured as her slave. He thought of the feelings of worthlessness and despair that had plagued him every day, and left him numb and powerless.

Just imagine it's her and do it.

The Doppelgänger regarded him with a crooked and amused smile.

'Dithering as usual, Ralph? Well, why not. After all, you know it's too late for her, don't you?'

Ralph stiffened.

'What do you mean?'

'Myrtle, the *other* Myrtle, will have got to her by now. She'll have wrung her neck good and proper, like I should have done to you. Like you, I left the decision too late.'

Ralph shook his head.

'You're lying. She's hidden, in the tunnels. Doppel Myrtle won't be able to find her. I'll go back and kill her, when I've done you in.'

He raised the dagger behind his head and readied himself to plunge it into the Doppelgänger's chest. But the Doppelgänger shook his head.

'"Doppel Myrtle"? How sweet. I suppose it helps to know who you're talking about. Shame you didn't think about that before.'

Ralph's hand stayed suspended. He could sense that something was wrong. What had he missed?

'You're lying again, to trick me, to save yourself.'

The Doppelgänger coughed and dark droplets of blood spattered across his chest.

'No, no, I'm telling the truth. You've got it all wrong. Your Myrtle's not in the tunnels, your Myrtle's in the chamber, tied up and strapped to the chest by the fire.'

'What?' Ralph's voice juddered. He let his arm fall.

'I caught her, you see, when I found her.'

'But Doppel Myrtle led you to the chamber. You don't know your way.'

The Doppelgänger let out a little sigh. 'That is true, I don't know my way around the tunnels. But luckily for me, you left a trail: a trail of your own blood.'

'My head!' exclaimed Ralph. He remembered how it had been bleeding all the way into the chamber when they had first arrived at the caves.

'Drop by drop, Ralph, I followed you. Of course, poor innocent Myrtle thought I was you. I didn't even know she had opened the box but she was so desperate to own up to what she had done, that she didn't bother to check who I was.'

'I should have branded you,' said Ralph.

'But you didn't. Anyway, Myrtle told me everything; how she opened the box while you were asleep, how she was knocked out by some strange force. I knew then that *Doppel Myrtle* must be somewhere in the tunnels.'

'But …' started Ralph and then it all became crystal clear. Doppel Myrtle had tricked him. Broken arm? Twisted ankle? Like hell! It was all a lie. He should have known. "It's just a scratch." Yes, a scratch she had inflicted on herself. He groaned. She even said she'd heard of Doppelgängers. But when he'd said 'Doppelgänger' earlier, in the chamber, she didn't know what he was talking about. And when he mentioned his promise, she didn't know about that either.

The Doppelgänger coughed again. His voice was weaker now but it dripped with malice. 'Yes Ralph, I made your poor innocent Myrtle call out for you. It's amazing what someone will do when they have a dagger at their back. And of course you came, like the puppy that you are.'

Ralph, reeling from the shock of the deception, from his own utter stupidity, just stood and stared at the gloating beast that lay before him.

'I expect your Myrtle will be as broken as I am by now. We show no mercy, you see. What will she think when she sees the blade coming for her? She'll wonder where you are. Why yet again you left her to die. After she saved your miserable life. You have to see the funny side, you snivelling little mouse.'

The Doppelgänger started to laugh.

With a cry of anguish Ralph brought the dagger down and thrust it straight into the monster's heart.

Chapter Fifteen

Bloodied, aching and exhausted, Ralph hauled himself back up the cliff with the rope.

How could I have been so stupid, he thought over and over. *I should have known. The real Myrtle wouldn't have said those things about giving up. The Doppelgänger was spurring me on, setting me up for the fight. She wanted me to go after my Doppelgänger so she could go after Myrtle.*

Numb to the core he clambered into the tunnel and lay for a second on the stony floor. Was there any chance at all that he could save her? He had to try. He staggered to his feet and limped away as fast as he could.

Ralph heard them before he saw them. The screeches were like knives in his ears. He ran, recklessly, at full pelt into the chamber to be confronted by an almighty fight. Myrtle and

Doppel Myrtle were entangled in a writhing, biting, clawing battle.

He could only stand and look on desperate to pitch in, but unable to distinguish between the two. And then in the midst of the fight, one of the Myrtles saw him. She was locked in a deadly embrace with her opponent. She looked at Ralph with those pleading eyes.

'Help me, Ralph. Get her off. Kill her, stab her, save me!'

He took a step forward, the bloodied dagger in his hand. But then the other Myrtle started up.

'No, help me, not her! It's me. Can't you see?'

But Ralph couldn't see. The two Myrtles fell to the ground and rolled back and forth in a tangle of arms and legs. If he had ever had even the smallest chance of telling the two apart, it was gone now. There was too much blood and dirt covering their faces.

'No!' he shouted and paced helplessly up and down. It was happening again. It was all going wrong. Myrtle, the real Myrtle, the girl who had saved his life, was going to die in front of him. And it was his stupid fault.

Suddenly, to his horror, one of the Myrtles gained the upper hand. *But which one?* She sat on top of the other, pinning her arms down with her knees, her hands around her victim's throat. She looked at Ralph.

'Ralph! Don't just stand there, come and help me! Hold down her legs. Can't you see? I'm the real Myrtle. I'm the one who saved you.'

Ralph looked desperately from one to the other. Which was which? Who was going to die and who was going to live?

The trapped girl struggled wildly. She couldn't speak. Her face was going purple. Her eyes were bulging. Her arms were pinned but she waved her hands about wildly, reaching out to Ralph, palms upwards in a gesture of pleading.

Ralph let out a cry of rage and darted forward. Two sets of eyes stared at him in terror. And for the second time his dagger found its fatal mark in the heart of evil.

Chapter Sixteen

Ralph took a long gulp of his steaming tea. He looked across at Myrtle and she managed a smile.

'Phew,' he whistled. 'Your neck looks sore.'

Myrtle rubbed at the bruises.

'I told you, I'm tougher than I look. It's funny, but my hand actually hurts much more.' She held out her right hand and Ralph saw that the burn mark from the poker had now blistered.

'You'll have a scar.'

She laughed.

'A brand, don't you mean?'

Ralph grinned, embarrassed.

'I know, I know. It was the Doppelgängers who should have been branded. But I suppose it didn't matter in the end. It was still the only way I could tell the two of you apart. When I saw the burn on your hand I knew that you were the real Myrtle.'

'The real Myrtle,' she repeated. 'You know, I like the sound of that.' She looked at Ralph curiously. 'If you hadn't seen my hand and the burn, what would you have done?

Which one of us would you have stabbed?'

Ralph shook his head slowly.

'I don't even want to think about it.'

They sipped their tea, both contemplating how badly things could have turned out.

'What was it like?' asked Myrtle suddenly. 'I mean what did it feel like, to kill them both?'

Ralph shook his head.

'I can't describe it. But I know it changes you, inside. I hope I never have to do it again.'

'I think we have both changed a little.' Myrtle nodded towards the body that lay on the far side of the chamber. 'What shall we do about that?'

'Hmm. I thought we could wheel her to the edge of the cliff and toss her over. I saw a pushcart down one of the tunnels that looks in okay shape.'

'Hah! A fitting burial, I think. And after that?'

Ralph shrugged.

'Let's pack up and go on down to the harbour and get on that ship.' He stood up. 'But there is just one thing I want to do first. In fact, let's get going now, before the tide is too high.'

Not long after, Ralph brought a dusty pushcart into the chamber and he and Myrtle loaded the Doppelgänger's body onto it. He pushed it through the passageways, Myrtle leading the way. He had a lantern though it was not needed. Myrtle, true to her word, knew every twist and turn in the dark. In fact, she took him a quicker route.

'What are you going to do with the black box?' she asked as they entered the final tunnel.

'I don't know. I should probably burn it, make sure this can't happen again.'

'Seems like a bit of a waste.'

Ralph shrugged. He wheeled the pushcart to the edge of the cliff and gave it a mighty shove. It seemed to hang in the air for a moment before vanishing out of sight. Ralph and Myrtle looked out together. The pushcart had shattered on the nearly submerged rocks and Doppel Myrtle was floating gently on the choppy sea.

'He's still down there' said Ralph meaningfully. The tide was not quite fully in yet and the Doppelgänger's body had been brought practically up to the cliff's edge. It lay on the sand just beyond the water's reach.

Ralph looked at Myrtle.

'There's still time.'

'If you want to do it, I'm not going to stop you,' she said.

Epilogue

In the depths of a winter's night, in a nameless coastal town, a lonely figure came trudging through the snow that lay on the roads. He was pushing a small cart, its load covered by a dirty blanket. This was not an easy task uphill on the rough, icy ground. The snow had long been hardened by the boots of passers-by and the traveller was panting heavily at the effort. He stopped for a moment to push back a part of the load that was dangling over the edge of the cart, and then trudged steadily on, like a beast of burden.

Soon he reached the top of the hill and entered the town square. He crossed it diagonally and turned off down Salter's Alley. He stopped under an old sign swinging on rusty chains. The peeling letters read:

The Smuggler's End
Tavern and Lodging House

The traveller knocked three times on the door, each knock as precise as the striking of the clock's hammer. There was no reply. He knocked again and a shout came from an overhead window.

'What's your game, lad? Can't you see we're closed? Come back in the morning!'

'But I got something for you,' the traveller called back, keeping his head down and muffling his voice with his scarf. 'Something important. There's money in it.'

The window slammed and from within the building there came the sound of heavy footsteps on the stairs. Moments later the door opened and the generous form of Mrs Ena Harbledown stood there with a flickering chamber candle. The landlady peered at the traveller.

'This had better be worth it,' she snapped. Her sleep-creased face was no less ugly for the feeble light.

'Judge for yourself,' he said.

In one quick movement he pulled the cover from the cart to reveal its load. Mrs Harbledown leaned over to see and let out a screech of horror.

There in the cart, crumpled almost beyond recognition, lay the bloodied, broken and very dead body of a boy. The moon shone down on the boy's mud-green eyes. And the eyes reflected nothing.

'It's the boy the constables are chasing. The one who murdered old man Doran. I believe there's a reward.'

Mrs Harbledown narrowed her puffy eyes suspiciously.

'And how would you come into possession of such a thing?'

'I caught him to prove my innocence, Mrs Harbledown.' The boy removed his hat and showed his face and the woman gasped.

'Ralph? Ralph Bennett? But how can it be? You were about to be hanged.'

'I told you, the murderer looked like me. Check for yourself.'

Mrs Harbledown stepped out into the snow and nervously folded down the lapels of the coat to reveal the bloodied face beneath.

'I suppose there's a resemblance. What happened to him?'

'He put up quite a fight. All you've got to say is that it's me. You'll get the reward.'

Mrs Harbledown pursed her lips. Apologies did not come easy to her. In fact, they did not come at all.

'It was an honest mistake. So much blood ...'

'Don't worry, I'm not here to cause trouble for you.'

Mrs Harbledown looked suspicious.

'What's in it for you?'

'I get to leave town and live my own life. I can't stay.'

'But does this mean you will want a share of the reward?'

Ralph shrugged.

'I just wanted you to know I was no murderer, that I wouldn't repay your kindness with such an evil act.'

'S'ppose that's fair,' said Mrs Harbledown, oblivious to any sarcasm. She thought for a moment. 'I could give you a few shillings, to help you on your way.'

Ralph smiled. 'Well, Mrs Harbledown, that is very generous of you. But, I hate to take money for nothing. You're welcome to the body for free, but I'll give you something in exchange for your shillings.' He held out a black box, a small shiny black box with buckles and a brass lock. Like a pirate's chest.

'Why, that's old man Doran's box,' she cried, her eyes gleaming.

'Maybe it'll bring you more luck than it brought me.'

Mrs Harbledown grabbed the box, her eyes widening as the box let off a soft glow. She examined it and gave it a shake.

'Oh, there's nothing in it,' said Ralph. 'I have a key too, but Mr Doran told me that you mustn't open it.'

'Really? How odd. Perhaps I should take the key, just in case …'

'As you wish.' Ralph handed it over and took a purse of coins in exchange. 'I'll be on my way then.'

'Probably best. You were good with them pigs, though.' said Mrs Harbledown. 'Look out for yourself now, Ralph.'

Ralph smiled as he walked off.

'Oh, I always do,' he said. 'I always do.'

The End

Seeing Double

Ghostly tales of real-life doppelgängers
By Christopher Edge

Imagine looking into a mirror late at night and then seeing your reflection step out of the glass to stand right in front of you. Say hello to your doppelgänger…

How to recognise your doppelgänger

The name *doppelgänger* comes from a German word meaning 'double walker'. A doppelgänger is an exact copy of a living person. However, unlike an identical twin, a doppelgänger is a supernatural creature or spirit – more like a ghost than a living human being.

The history of doppelgängers

Many countries and cultures have believed in ghostly doubles like the doppelgänger:

- The ancient Egyptians called this 'spirit double' a *ka*: a ghostly copy of a person who lived in a special type of tomb. In order to make sure the ghostly double didn't escape from the tomb and wander the earth, priests would leave offerings of food and drink to keep the ka happy.

- In Scandinavian countries, there are legends of doppelgängers who appear at places before the person they are a copy of actually arrives. This can cause quite a fright at parties if the real person shows up and their doppelgänger is already on the dancefloor!

- The legend of the doppelgänger has also been linked to the many stories of monks, saints and holy men. Friar Padre Pio was a monk in Southern Italy during World War II. He promised to protect residents of San Giovanni from harm. When a fleet of American bombers attacked the town, Padre Pio appeared in the air in front of the pilots to stop them releasing their bombs. However, at the same time, he was still in his Friary on the ground!

My teacher is a doppelgänger!

In 1845, Emilie Sagée was a 32-year-old French teacher who taught in an exclusive girls' school. One day when she was writing on the blackboard at the front of the classroom, her exact double appeared beside her, copying her every movement. The students in the classroom were astounded to see a doppelgänger of their teacher, but Miss Sagée didn't notice a thing.

Soon other sightings of Miss Sagée's doppelgänger were reported around the school.

- In the school dinner hall, Miss Sagée's doppelgänger could be seen standing behind her. The doppelgänger seemed to be eating in exactly the same way as Miss Sagée, even though it didn't have a knife or fork.

- When Miss Sagée was teaching in her classroom, her doppelgänger could be spotted in different parts of the school.

- Once Miss Sagée's doppelgänger appeared in front of an entire class of students who were seated in the school hall, even though the real Miss Sagée could be seen through the window in the school garden. When two daring students approached the doppelgänger, they felt a strange force blocking their path. Then, one of the girls stepped through Miss Sagée's ghostly figure as if it wasn't there and the doppelgänger slowly faded away.

Although Emilie Sagée never saw her own doppelgänger, whenever it appeared she found herself feeling strangely drained. Her movements became much slower and her skin turned pale until her ghostly double disappared again.

Nobody ever heard Miss Sagée's doppelgänger speak, but word of its appearances spread fear throughout the school. Parents withdrew their daughters from her classes and eventually the school was forced to fire Miss Sagée. From that day on, her doppelgänger was never seen in the school again, but some say it followed Miss Sagée to her grave.

Doppelgänger danger

Seeing a doppelgänger is thought to be very bad luck. If your friends spot your doppelgänger, then it might mean that something terrible is about to happen to you. However, it could be even worse. Seeing your own doppelgänger is supposed to be a sign that you are about to die.

These people saw their own doppelgänger and didn't live to tell the tale:

- In 1822, the poet Percy Bysshe Shelley met his own doppelgänger a month before he drowned.

- The American president Abraham Lincoln said that he saw his doppelgänger on the eve of his election. He looked into a mirror and saw two faces staring back at him, one face much paler than the other. When Abraham Lincoln told his wife what he had seen, she said that it was a sign that he would win the election but wouldn't live long enough to see out his full term of office. Lincoln was shot dead by an assassin less than five years later.

- Queen Elizabeth I saw an image of her doppelgänger lying ill on her deathbed only a few days before she died herself.

- Writer Guy de Maupassant met his own doppelgänger in strange and sinister circumstances. When he locked himself in a room to write a new story, he was surprised by a visitor: his doppelgänger! Sitting in a chair, the writer's doppelgänger started to dictate a tale about an evil spirit who haunted his victim and drove him insane. Guy de Maupassant wrote the story down, but when it was finally published the author himself was sent mad and died an early death, just as his doppelgänger's story predicted!

Strange explanations

What might cause someone to think they have seen a doppelgänger?

In some religions people believe that a person's spirit can travel outside of their body. This is called 'astral travelling'. So if you spot someone out and about when you think they're at home asleep, this might just be their spirit popping out astral travelling!

Scientific researchers, however, have a different theory. They have conducted experiments that show that stimulating a certain part of a person's brain you can make them think they had seen a ghostly double by their side. So if you think you've spotted your own doppelgänger, don't worry! You might just be wearing your hat too tightly on your head...

We would like to thank the following schools and students for all their help in developing and trialling *The Perfect Enemy*:

Queensbridge School

Hasan Ali
Farees Almatari
Faisal Alwarey
Tyler Blair-Thompson
Max Bradbury
Shahid Farooq
Nazmul Haque
Rayhan Hussain
Umayr Hussain
Jameelah Ibrahim
Umer Khan
Ehsaan Lal
Henrique Lambertini
Ihtishaam Majid
Junayd Munir
Destiny Omoigui
Samuel Pemberton
Sophie Pinnegar
Zakariya Rahman
Aaron Reatus
Jamie-Lee Smith
Roche Smith
Saqib Ul-Hassan
Chulothe Urooj
Oliver Watkins
Ithsham Yasin
Raakib Zaman

Discover all the titles in the
HEROES series at

**www.pearsonschools.co.uk/
HEROES**.

Dark, daring, heroic.